HOLE JOE

MARY BLAKESLEE

Other books by Mary Blakeslee

It's Tough to Be a Kid
Halfbacks Don't Wear Pearls
Carnival
Edythe with a Y
Outta Sight
Chocolate Pie for Breakfast
It's Still Tough to Be a Kid
Museum Mayhem
Rodeo Rescue
Will to Win
Say Cheese!

MARY BLAKESLEE

HOLY JOE

Stoddart

Irwin Young Adult Fiction is an imprint of
Stoddart Publishing Co. Limited.

First published in 1990 by
Stoddart Publishing Co. Limited
34 Lesmill Road
Toronto, Canada
M3B 2T6

CANADIAN CATALOGUING IN PUBLICATION DATA

Blakeslee, Mary
    Holy Joe

ISBN 0-7737-2339-0 (bound)   ISBN 0-7737-5343-5 (pbk.)

I. Title.

PS8553.L348H6 1990   jC813'.54   C89-090618-1
PZ7.B53Ho 1990

Cover design: Brant Cowie/ArtPlus Limited
Illustration: Tony Meers
Typesetting: Tony Gordon Ltd.
Printed in Canada

To Betty Gibb,
with love

One

"For what we are about to receive, may the Lord make us truly thankful. Amen."

"Amen."

"Amen."

"Amen. Yuck, it'd take more than the Lord to make us thankful for this!"

My sister, Marty, peered down at the bowl my mother handed her and gagged dramatically.

"That will be enough, Mary Martha," our father ordered. "Mrs. Granger very kindly sent that over to us, and I will not have you speak ill of such a charitable gesture."

Marty passed the odious bowl down to me and grabbed a piece of bread. I checked out the contents cautiously. The green stuff covering the bottom of the bowl looked like stewed shoelaces swimming in seaweed. Another of Lucy Granger's generous contributions to the preacher's family. I took a small helping and covered it in catsup, hoping to disguise the taste. Mom watched me and grinned.

"Here, Joe, have some salad. It's guaranteed not to cause acute gastritis."

"Marcella, please don't encourage the children in their lack of gratitude. Mrs. Granger is only trying to help."

"She could help a lot more," Mom snapped, "if she'd use her influence as a board member of the church to increase your salary instead of sending care packages over to us." She picked up the offending bowl and ladled out the remainder of the shoelaces onto Dad's plate.

"Here you are. Enjoy." Then she got up from the table and went into the kitchen. A few minutes later she returned with a platter of scrambled eggs in her hand and a make-my-day look on her face.

I glanced over at Dad to see how he was taking this palace revolt. He was ignoring us all as he valiantly spooned up Mrs. Granger's unidentifiable mess and grimly pushed it down with slices of bread.

"Very tasty," he murmured stoically, and stuffed a thick crust into his mouth.

Marty and Mom burst into a fit of giggles and I dared a small smile. Dad glared at us and kept on eating.

Another typical Sunday afternoon at the home of the Reverend Dr. Rupert Larriby and his family.

Fortunately, Mrs. Granger's charity didn't run to desserts, so we finished the meal in style with one of Mom's totally decadent chocolate creations. By the time we'd demolished a whole mocha soufflé, Dad was in a much better mood.

"Well, time to get back to the church. Young People's starts in less than an hour." He got up from the table, stretched, and smiled at Mom. "Lovely dinner, my dear. You must make that again sometime."

I wasn't sure whether he meant the soufflé or the seaweed. Dad's memory leaves a lot to be desired at times, so it could be that he'd already forgotten about

Mrs. Granger's donation — and how totally repulsive it was.

Mom just nodded pleasantly and began to clear the table.

"Come, Joseph, you can walk over to the church with me," Dad suggested. "There's a bit of setting up to do, and I suspect Stan might have taken off for the day."

Stan is the old guy who does odd jobs around the church, like putting out chairs and seeing that the cat hasn't left any mice on the altar; that is, when he's sober enough he does them. Everyone wonders why Dad keeps him around, but he just quotes that bit about his brother's keeper and tries to keep Stan from mooning the Ladies Aid when he's in his cups.

I stood up and took a deep breath. "Dad," I began, my voice too loud as I tried to sound casual, "I don't think I'll go to Young People's this afternoon." There — it was out and the ceiling hadn't fallen on my head.

"Don't make jokes about the church, Joseph," Dad admonished me. "It's tasteless."

"I wasn't joking," I replied. "I really don't want to go to Young People's today — maybe never again. I'm almost eighteen and the oldest guy in the group. Practically everyone else quits when they reach sixteen," I finished lamely.

Dad stared at me as if I'd announced I was planning to join the Hare Krishnas and spend the rest of my life in airports. "Joseph, what are you saying?" He dropped back into his chair and stared at me. "Why, next thing you'll be telling me you want to resign from the choir."

That had crossed my mind, but I figured one bomb at a time was enough.

The best thing right now, I decided, was to keep my

mouth shut. I knew how I was hurting Dad by wanting to give up one of his pet church activities, but I was determined that this time I wasn't going to give in. Sunday afternoon was the time when the Creature Comforts practiced.

I've never been a big social success in school — or out, for that matter. Until last year I looked like an ad for Save the Children: five five and 120. Then I took a sudden growth spurt and ended up topping six two and weighing in at 185. Since then, my peers, as they say, have begun to look at me in a different light.

Particularly Amy Hubank.

Anyway, when school started a few weeks ago I was suddenly invited to join a couple of clubs, the football coach eyed me greedily, and the Creature Comforts asked me to sing lead and play rhythm guitar. The last is not as surprising at you might think. I've been singing in our church choir since I was about five, and since I started soloing at weddings for junk-food and movie money I've got a reputation for having a pretty decent voice.

But to join the Creature Comforts I'd have to give up Young People's, the teenage group from our church. I'd belonged since I was thirteen and at one time really enjoyed it. I guess the reason was that I was going through the religious phase that every kid experiences along with erotic fantasies and zits. Mine lasted longer than most, what with my father being a minister in the town of Hubank (pop. 54,870, named after its founder, Elias P. Hubank — Amy's great-grandfather — seven churches, one synagogue; main industry: chewing gum factory; Rotary meets every Wednesday).

Anyway, I was fed up to my Adam's apple with Young People's and their boring activities. The most exciting thing we did last year was collect beer bottles to sell so we could sponsor a guy to come in and speak to us on the evils of drink.

I ask you!

However, I didn't want to hurt Dad. He's the sweetest, gentlest guy in the world; he makes Gandhi look like Conan the Barbarian. The problem is he's still living back in the nineteenth century when fun on Sunday was sitting around the pump organ singing hymns and praying for those sinners who played cards and danced on the Sabbath.

I cleared my throat and tried for firmness.

"The thing is, I've been asked to join a rock group. They practice Sunday afternoons."

"A rock group?" He made it sound like white slavery, and I knew I was going to need some help. I shot Mom a pleading look.

"I think Joe is right, dear," she offered, picking up her cue. "After all, Marty will be starting Young People's in a couple of weeks when she turns thirteen, and I'm sure Joe wouldn't feel comfortable in the same group as his younger sister."

Marty's face took on the same expression it had when she'd seen Mrs. Granger's stew.

"But a rock group!" Dad exclaimed, ignoring Marty's frantic head-shaking. "They smoke illegal cigarettes and take chemical stimulants."

"Dad," I pleaded, trying not to smile, "there's nothing in the constitution that says you have to take drugs to play rock. The Creature Comforts are very straight. As a matter of fact, Amy Hubank plays keyboard for them."

"She does?" He looked momentarily taken aback. "So that's why I never see her around the church anymore." He rose from the chair and stretched up to his full six foot three. "I must have a word with her parents. I'm sure they are unaware that she has slipped from grace."

"Oh, for heaven's sake, Rupert!" Mom cried. "When are you going to join us in the eighties? The Hubanks know all about the band and quite approve of Amy being involved. It's wonderful experience for her; and it will be equally wonderful for Joe." She crumpled up a paper napkin, brushed a few crumbs off the table, and left the room.

Dad stood there looking baffled for a moment or so, then shrugged his shoulders.

"I suppose your mother knows best, Joseph," he sighed. "She usually does, it seems." He went off muttering something about worldly pleasures and the good old days.

I looked at Marty and grinned.

She didn't grin back.

"Does he really think I'm going to spend the better part of my adolescence cooped up in the church basement listening to Harry Gruber's adenoids and watching Nora Wells comb her hair? Honestly, Joe, I don't know how you've stood it all these years."

"It wasn't that bad." I figured I could be magnanimous now that I was out of it.

"Maybe not for you. After all, Saralee Tidbell was in the group," she answered with a mocking grin.

Saralee Tidbell. I'd been paired with her since we were both in the nursery during church services. Even when I was a ninety-pound weakling and the guy voted most unlikely to succeed I resented Saralee Tidbell. She looks like Peewee Herman and has the personality of a parking meter. And she fawns.

I didn't bother arguing. Marty isn't so dumb that she'd think I could possibly be interested in Saralee. She was just angry because she was expected to take over where I left off at Young People's. I knew, however, that would never happen. Unlike me, Marty has never given in to anyone or anything she didn't like.

When I was eight I was expected to join a Cub pack. When Marty was eight and ready for Brownies, the pre-Girl Guide gang, she announced that she wouldn't have time for that sort of nonsense; she and her girlfriends were going to start publishing their own newspaper: The Hubank Hustler.

Dad was very upset, not because of the name — I'm pretty sure he's never opened a copy of the original Hustler in his entire life. He thinks Playboy is a games magazine for little kids. But there wasn't much he could do about it beyond dragging her bodily to the Brownie meetings. So Marty published her paper every two weeks for about a year and made more money than I was making as bag boy at Granger's Grocery.

Marty also got out of Girl Guides and piano lessons and choir and about everything else she didn't like.

And Dad let her do it.

It's not that he doesn't care what Marty does: he's strict about a lot of things, but I guess he figures it's Mom's responsibility to oversee Marty's social life.

I, on the other hand, am a different matter. I'm expected to play the role of the preacher's son — as an example to my peers, Dad argues. So I do — or did.

But since the beginning of this year I'd been feeling different about this role. I figured I was about ready to start my very own, very small rebellion.

Two

So I took my first rebellious step. At first it felt good, then I started thinking about Dad going to the church and having to set up all alone and the good feeling slipped away. As a matter of fact, I almost gave in and went with him, but Mom came to my rescue just in time.

"He'll be fine, Joe," she assured me, coming back into the dining room and seeing me sitting there looking guilty. "Your father only wants what's best for you, you know. The problem is, his concept of what's best is a bit old-fashioned. Now, get rid of any ideas about backing out of your decision. It's time you became more involved in school and community activities."

"Amen!" Marty exclaimed. "It sure is a drag to have a brother everybody calls *Holy Joe*."

"Oh, no! Really?" Mom shot her an amazed look.

"Really." Then to me, Marty said, "Honestly, Joe, you've got so much on the ball. You shouldn't be wasting it."

I got up from the table and smiled at both of them. "Okay, little sister, you're right. And thanks for understanding, Mom. I just hope Dad can."

I left the room, picked up my guitar, and went to the practice.

* * *

The Creature Comforts practice in Gord Lindsay's rec room. Gord plays drums and is the founder and therefore leader of the group. When I got to Gord's house a little after two, the rest of the band was already there: Ellis LaCroy, lead guitar; Mac Kuschner, bass, and of course Amy Hubank on keyboard. The Creature Comforts started a couple of years ago, playing at school dances and the odd commercial affair. The original band consisted of Gord, Ellis, Mac, and Margie Manson. Amy joined the group a year ago, and when Margie graduated last spring they needed a replacement; that's where I came in.

"Hey, good you could make it," Gord greeted me as I stood at the top of the stairs leading down to the rec room. "Get on down here. We're just about ready to begin."

I started down the stairs and in my nervousness managed to fall down the last three steps. Mac and Ellis looked at each other and shrugged. Amy gave me an encouraging smile and I got to an empty chair without further mishap.

I'm pretty good on the guitar, so I was able to hold my own when Gord got us going on an old Abba number. But when it came time for me to sing I practically fell apart. My voice was weak and I missed an easy high note.

When I finally finished I was pretty sure the group was going to ask me to leave, but instead Gord grinned and said, "Don't sweat it, Joe. You're among friends."

Mac and Ellis shrugged.

I did a lot better on the next couple of numbers as I began to lose some of my nervousness. When we finally packed it up about four o'clock I really felt I had been accepted and was a genuine member of a great rock group.

"A bunch of kids are coming over to my house tonight, Joe," Amy said as we were packing up our instruments. "I'd like it if you could be there." She gave me a smile that had more wattage than Ellis's amplifier, and I could feel my blood pressure rocketing.

"Gee, that would be great, Amy," I answered when my mouth started working again. I was just about to ask what time when I realized it was Sunday. Evening service at the church. "Oh, no, I just remembered; I have to . . ." Go to church? Now wouldn't that just turn her right on! " . . . go to a meeting," I finished cryptically.

"Oh, that's too bad. I'm sorry." Amy's mouth turned down at the corners. She looked as if she really *was* sorry. Not half as sorry as I was, though. "Maybe another time." She gave me that electric smile again and added, "Want to walk me home? We go the same way."

Before I could answer her, Mac and Ellis came over and took her arms. "Come on, Amy. Let's get a pizza."

Amy looked at me, then back at them. "Okay, but you come too, Joe."

Mac and Ellis shrugged. I was beginning to think that's how they communicated; they've got it down to a fine art. So the four of us said goodbye to Gord and left together.

We were walking down the street toward the pizza parlor, Amy and I in front and Mac and Ellis behind. Amy was telling me all about the music scholarship she was trying for to go to Juilliard. She played keyboard in the group but her real love was piano. She hoped to make it as a concert pianist, although, she admitted, her chances were pretty slim.

"Only one in thousands makes it to the top," she explained, "but I want to give it a shot anyway."

I was nodding encouragingly and staring down at her perfect profile, too overwhelmed by everything that was happening to me to do much more than mumble inanities.

"And what do you want to do with your life, Joe, or do you know yet?"

"What? Me?" I managed to tear my eyes off Amy and get my tongue working again. "I'm not sure, but I think I'd like to make music my life too. Oh, not that I have your talent, of course, but I think I could be good enough to make it with a good commercial group."

"You've got a great voice, Joe. I used to get goose pimples when I heard you sing in church. Matter of fact, it was me that suggested you to Gord for the band."

"You? Gee, Amy, I didn't know." I stared down at her again, feeling my heart pound as if I'd just done a hundred push-ups. I noticed for the first time that she had exactly seven freckles across the top of her nose and that when she smiled, a little dimple appeared on her left cheek. I think it's called falling in love.

I guess that's why I didn't see Saralee Tidbell until she was nearly on top of us.

"Well, for heaven's sake, Joey," she gushed as she blocked the sidewalk in front of us. "Imagine meeting you here. I thought you must be sick since you weren't at Young People's this afternoon." She smiled broadly and stood her ground. When Saralee Tidbell smiles she shows about six inches of upper gums. It's like watching a chimpanzee trying to attract a mate. I know that's a little unkind, but Saralee brings out the worst in me. And at that moment she was the last person in the world I wanted to see.

"I don't go to Young People's anymore," I answered shortly and moved to the side to pass her. I took Amy's arm and began walking quickly away. I thought I was home free when Saralee called out from behind us.

"See you tonight at church service, Joey. I'll save you a seat."

I felt Amy's arm stiffen under my hand. Then from behind I heard Mac whisper to Ellis, "Holy Joe." I didn't have to look back to see them shrugging.

* * *

"You still go to church twice on Sundays?" Amy asked as we settled into a booth and waited for the waitress to take our orders.

"Sometimes," I hedged. "Dad sort of expects it of the family. The united front and all that."

The three of them looked at me and seemed to be waiting for me to go on. I shrugged and tried to look nonchalant. "I think that's very nice," Amy said, rescuing me. "I used to go Sunday evenings too, until I started to get behind in chem and had to be tutored. Then I just sort of didn't go back when the tutoring was over."

I shot her a grateful glance and took a gulp of water. Before the guys could ask any more questions, the waitress sidled up to the booth, flipping the pages of her order pad, and I was taken off the hook. At least for the time being.

"Were you there when Gord told us about the job he

got for us to play at the Elks Halloween dance?" Amy asked as she bit into her double-cheese/hold-the-anchovies slice of pizza.

"No," I answered. "Must have been before I got there. Is that good?"

"The best," Mac said with a nod. "It could be the break we've been waiting for. Everybody goes to the Elks dance. When they see how good we are, we could be looking at more gigs than we can handle."

"That's why Gord insists we start practicing every evening until the dance," Ellis explained. "We're good now, but we've got to be the best."

"Every evening?" The pepperoni I was chewing suddenly turned to Silly Putty.

"Right. And weekends. We can do our homework after school," Ellis continued. "But it looks like our social life will be pretty bleak until November."

"Oh, well, all in a good cause." Amy grinned. "It's the price we have to pay to be the hottest band in the county."

I didn't say anything, but no one seemed to notice my silence. They were all so high on the idea of really making it big, I guess. I sat looking down at my half-eaten pizza and wondered what I was going to do.

In the first place, I had a job Saturdays. I'd been promoted from bag boy at Granger's Grocery to delivery boy. It paid pretty well and it was my contribution to the family fund. Not that Mom or Dad had asked me to help out, but a minister's salary doesn't buy a lot of extras. In fact, in Dad's case, it hardly bought all the essentials. Mom wasn't able to work, what with all the duties she was expected to perform as the minister's wife. Besides, she was a flight attendant before she was married, and there aren't too many calls for forty-one-year-old women in that business.

In the second place, choir practice was on Tuesday evenings. I had planned to give that up sometime in the future when Dad had got used to my opting out of Young People's, but now it looked as if I'd have to quit immediately. That is, if I wanted to stay in the group.

"What's the matter, Joe?" Amy asked, looking down at my half-eaten pizza. "Are you feeling okay? You look kind of weird."

"Huh? Oh, I'm fine. Just thinking about a couple of things." I bit into my pizza and forced myself to swallow. This was just one more problem I'd have to face, and I'd find some way to resolve it, I promised myself. But not right now.

I took a couple more bites of pizza and glanced at my watch.

"Hey, I'd better get moving," I muttered. "It's almost five and we eat at five-thirty on Sunday nights." I checked the bill, put a couple of bucks on the table, and rose. "Guess I'll see you in class tomorrow," I said, looking down at Amy.

"And at practice, of course." Her eyes were brimming with laughter as she looked at me. "Have a good *meeting*," she said and squeezed my hand.

Ellis and Mac . . . well, I'm sure you know what Ellis and Mac did.

Three

*H*ow was practice?" Mom asked brightly as I came into the kitchen a few minutes later.

She and Dad were getting supper ready — at least she was; Dad was more or less setting the table and generally getting in Mom's way. We always eat Sunday supper at the kitchen table to save time. The *day of rest* just doesn't seem to have enough hours in it to get everything done.

"It was great!" I answered as I snatched a stalk of celery from the relish tray. "We've been invited to play at the Elks Halloween dance."

"My, that *is* impressive." Mom stopped scraping carrots and looked over at me. "Is the band really that good?"

"Somebody seems to think so. It means a lot of practicing, of course." Somehow I was going to have to tell Dad I'd be quitting choir, and this seemed like a pretty good lead into it.

I should have known better.

"Well, as long as it doesn't interfere with your church work, I guess it will be all right," he said, "although I don't entirely approve of you staying out to all hours playing for these rowdy functions."

"Rupert, the Elks dances are the highlight of the social season," Mom chided him. "Everyone goes to them; they're the height of respectability. And I'm sure Joe's practicing won't interfere with his other duties."

I decided I wouldn't bother mentioning that we would be practicing every evening as well as Saturday afternoon. I'd worry about what I would do about choir practice and my job when the time came to make a decision.

The time came a lot faster than I'd anticipated.

* * *

We'd practiced Monday evening for a couple of hours. Gord had decreed that we wouldn't go past nine-thirty so we wouldn't get any flak from our parents or our teachers about taking too much time away from our schoolwork. I had planned to casually announce that I wouldn't be able to make it the next night. I didn't think one miss would make that much difference, and I needed a little time to make my break from choir practice. But before I had a chance to say anything, Gord dropped the bomb.

"Tomorrow night is really special, guys, so I want you all to be at your best. The man from the Elks who hired us is coming over to hear us play."

"Why does he want to do that?" Amy asked. "I thought the deal was all sewed up."

"Well, it is — practically. We haven't signed anything yet, and — well, it seems there's another group that they're looking at. This guy coming over tomorrow is going to make the final decision."

Amy and the other two groaned. Then Amy stood up and glared down at Gord, who was still sitting behind his drums.

"You should have told us this in the first place."

"I didn't know about the other group. I swear." Gord looked as stricken as I felt. "I was just as surprised as you when he told me we had competition."

Amy's anger visibly subsided and she slumped back into her seat. "Do you know who the other group is?"

"Yeah. The Sinful Six."

"They're good," Mac muttered.

"But not as good as we are," Gord cried. He jumped up and began striding up and down the room. "We'll show 'em. Tomorrow night I expect us to play like we've never played before. So everybody go home, get a good night's sleep, eat your Wheaties, and I'll see you here tomorrow night. Seven sharp."

So much for my missing one little practice.

* * *

I thought all the next day about how I would spring the news on Dad that I wouldn't be attending choir practice that night. In fact I was so spaced out trying to come up with the perfect excuse that I missed half the questions on a surprise quiz Mr. Donald gave us in algebra, my best subject. When Mr. Donald had us score one anothers' papers and the guy behind me announced I'd scored forty-seven percent everybody looked at me as though I'd grown another head.

"What's with you, Joe?" Woody asked as we headed for the caf at the end of the class. "You've never got less than a ninety in any math test since you learned to add single-column figures." He gave me a queer look and added, "You're not in love, are you?"

"Huh?" I asked, only half listening to him. Then what he said hit me. "Why? Does it show that much?"

"Then you *are* in love." He sounded kind of sad —

or maybe *envious* is a better word. "Who's the lucky girl?"

"If you must know, it's Amy Hubank."

"Wow! You're really hitting the big time, aren't you? Does she know how you feel about her?"

"No, I don't think so. Anyway, that's not what's bugging me right now."

We found seats at a corner table and started to dig into our brown bags.

"Okay then, give," Woody ordered, biting into his sandwich.

Wilfred "Woody" Albert has been my best friend since first grade. We used to do everything together because, to be honest, no one else paid much attention to us. Then when I had this growth spurt and started growing hair on my face I got popular, but Woody stayed pretty much the same: five four, skinny, glasses. He'll be a good-looking guy when he fills out and the rest of his face catches up with his nose. Meanwhile, I'm getting invited into the clubs and Woody is still the outsider. It's very difficult for both of us. But he's still my best friend and I still tell him everything.

"It's this rock band I've joined, Woody. We're playing at the Elks dance — at least it looks like we are."

"So what's the big problem with that? I wouldn't mind being in a rock group."

"It's not that," I sighed. "The thing is we have to practice every night. As you may remember, I have choir practice tonight."

"Can't you miss band practice just this once?"

I explained about the guy coming to audition us.

"Then can't you miss choir practice?"

"Woody, you know Dad. He's ticked off at me now for quitting Young People's; if I told him I was leaving the choir he'd have a coronary."

"You quit Young People's? For good?" He sounded downright brokenhearted. "I missed you on Sunday, but I just figured you must have been sick or something."

"Yeah, well, I had to quit. We practice every Sunday afternoon. Besides, I figured I was getting too old for it."

Cool move. Now Woody really looked hurt.

"So what are you going to do?" he asked halfheartedly.

"I've considered drinking toilet-bowl cleaner but that's so final. I guess I'll just have to try explaining to Dad how important this particular practice is and hope he'll understand."

About that time a couple of guys from Chi Delta, the illegal high school fraternity, came over to the table and sat down.

"Hey, Joe," Cliff Fortana, BMOC and president of said fraternity greeted me, "have you thought over what we talked about the other day?"

I gave Woody an uncomfortable look and muttered, "Sure, Cliff. The thing is, I've got to spend all my time with the Creature Comforts for the next little while."

"Yeah, I hear you landed the Elks dance," Sam Quan commented. "Nice going."

"You don't have to give us your answer right away, Joe, but we'd like to know pretty soon. We're initiating the new brothers the first week in October."

He got up and Sam followed suit. They both looked down at me, totally ignoring Woody, and smiled. "We'd really like to have you," Cliff said, implying that I'd be out of my skull if I wouldn't really like to be had. "So think it over carefully, eh?"

I nodded uncomfortably and they left to return to the exclusive table they reserved for the fraternity.

"You didn't tell me the Chi Delts had asked you to pledge!" Woody said as soon as they were out of earshot.

"I didn't think it was important," I muttered and began to pack up my garbage.

"Important! Who are you kidding, Joe?" He glared at me, then dropped his eyes and kind of sighed. "I suppose you're going to accept, but you could have at least told me about it."

"I hadn't decided," I answered.

The truth is, I didn't tell Woody because I knew he'd react just exactly as he had. Besides, I really hadn't decided whether to accept their invitation. Sure, it was a real prestige thing, and I'd be part of the in group that I'd always envied. But there was Woody to consider. If I joined the Chi Delts, would it break us up? And what about the time it would take from all my other commitments?

Then there was Dad. I was pretty sure he wouldn't approve of joining a fraternity. I could just hear him.

"It's undemocratic, Joseph. I wouldn't mind you affiliating with a club that accepted anyone who wished to join, but fraternities don't follow that principle. They pick and choose whom they think is worthy of the honor bestowed upon them. I don't believe in such behavior. It's not only undemocratic, it's unchristian!"

The final indisputable argument.

Geez! I thought. Being popular could ruin your life!

"Come on, let's get out of here," I said, trying to sound cheerful. "How about a little one-on-one? We've got half an hour before class."

"Naw," Woody answered. "It's no fun anymore. You're ten feet taller than me; I can't keep up."

"That's nuts, Woody. You're the fastest guy I've ever seen on the basketball court. I don't know why you won't try out for the team."

He gave me a disgusted look and didn't answer.

A flash of anger shot through me. Damn it all, it wasn't my fault that the Chi Delts hadn't asked Woody to join. And it sure wasn't my fault he hadn't grown. But he didn't seem to want to do anything for himself anymore. I was getting that claustrophobic feeling I sometimes got around Dad when he found fifteen things, all related to the church, for me to do.

The anger passed a moment later, and I grinned at him.

"Okay then. You wanna go over to the arcade and play a couple of games?"

Woody was a whiz at Galaga. When we were in junior high we both used to spend most of our allowance and all our free time playing the game, but that was three years ago. I'd outgrown the mindless activity, but it was the one thing Woody thought he excelled in, so I kept going along with him. After all, he *is* my best friend.

So we went over to the arcade; Woody topped his personal best, and we got back to the school just before the last bell.

I still hadn't figured out what to do about choir practice or the Chi Delts.

Four

I don't care what you do to me. You can shave my head, make me eat snakes, pull out my toenails; I still won't go to Young People's."

Marty's mouth was a thin line and her eyes flashed fire. Dad just looked helplessly at her, then at Mom.

"Perhaps if you tried it just once you might enjoy it," Mom coaxed.

We all knew it was useless. When Marty makes up her mind, heavenly bolts of lightning can't change it.

We were sitting around the dining room table finishing dinner when Dad mentioned that the Young People's group was having a party on Saturday night to welcome the new kids who would be joining this fall. It wasn't the subject I was most comfortable with, but I didn't think it would have all that much effect on me. Boy! Was I wrong!

"I have no intention of trying it," Marty answered Mom. "Even Holy Joe finally realized what a bunch of nerds they are."

"Marty, that is no way to refer to your brother." Dad's glasses were steaming and his face had turned pink. "Just because Joseph chooses to engage in church activities instead of tearing around the country doing heaven knows what is no excuse for you to make sport of him."

"He quit Young People's, don't forget."

"Only because he felt he was too old for the group. But he is still a loyal member of the choir; he still attends Sunday services; he still helps old Stan with chores. You might do half as well."

"Joe's different," Marty retorted. "After all, he's going into the ministry. I'm not."

Oh, God, I thought. Not this on top of everything else.

When I was quite young I had it all figured out that I would be a minister like Dad. It was at that time in my life when my old man was a superhero to me and I wanted to be just like him. Since then I'd had second thoughts. As a matter of fact, I wasn't even sure I wanted to go to university. As I told Amy, I was thinking I might make a career with my music. But I'd never come right out and told Dad any of this. Although I'd hinted often enough that I wasn't sure about theology as a profession, Dad just wouldn't take me seriously.

Now Marty had to bring this up just when I was going to tell Dad I wouldn't be at choir. There was no way now that I could do it.

On the other hand, if I missed band, Gord would probably hang me from the nearest rafter by my guitar strings. And I wouldn't blame him. I had only one choice.

* * *

"On your way to choir, dear?" Mom asked as I came downstairs an hour later.

"Just leaving," I answered, nicely dodging the

question. I checked to see that no one was in the living room, then slipped into the foyer, picked up my guitar, which I had carefully stashed in the hall closet, and hurried out the door.

Fortunately, Dad makes a point of not going to the church when the choir is practicing. This all came about five years ago when the new choir director was appointed. Dad showed up at his first rehearsal and made a few suggestions about the anthem and who should sing the solo part the following Sunday. Dunn Morgan, the choir director, made it quite clear that if Dad stuck around giving advice he could darn well lead the choir himself. Mr. Morgan is a Welshman with a great voice and all the charm of Idi Amin. Anyway, I didn't have to worry about getting caught, unless, of course, Dunn the Hun happened to mention to Dad that I was among the missing on Tuesday night.

I got to Gord's just as Amy was getting out of her dad's car, so we went into the house together.

"I'm so nervous I can hardly breathe," she murmured and took my hand as we headed for the rec room. "I just know I'll forget where all the keys are."

I grinned down at her. "That's nuts, Amy. You're a pro; you'll do just fine." Holding her hand made me forget all about sneaking out of choir and my own fear of performing in front of our potential client. Her hand was so soft and slender and her hair smelled like strawberries. It was a very heavy experience.

* * *

Mr. Bryce, the guy from the Elks, seemed to be happy with what he heard but he wasn't making any commitment, he said, until he'd checked out the Sinful Six. He'd let us know by the end of the week.

"We'll just continue on the assumption that we're in, and go ahead with our practice schedule as planned," Gord informed us when Bryce had left. Meanwhile, I think that's enough for tonight. We're all a little psyched out, so I don't think there's much point in pushing it." He stood up and stretched. "Anyone want to go for a Coke?"

"Sure, I guess so," Mac said and looked at Ellis. Ellis shrugged.

"I'm afraid I can't tonight," Amy responded. "Too much homework." She turned to me and continued, "Joe is going to help me with my algebra, aren't you, Joe?"

It was the first time I'd heard about it, but I wasn't quite stupid enough to blow it.

"Yeah, sure." I wondered just what Amy had in mind. "Maybe we'd better get going. There's a lot to cover."

Amy grinned and took my hand again. I was about two feet off the ground as we climbed the stairs and went out of the house.

* * *

"How was practice?" Mom asked from the living room where she and Dad were sitting together on the couch watching something zoological on PBS.

"Fine," I answered noncommittally. I wasn't lying. Practice *was* fine. I just didn't bother to mention which one.

"You had a couple of phone calls while you were out, Joe," Dad mumbled, not taking his eyes from the pregnant baboon. "I put the numbers on the bulletin board."

I left them to their primate studies and went out to check the phone calls.

The first was from Woody. "Call the minute you come in. Urgent." That could mean either he'd won a lottery or his gerbil had had babies. Woody doesn't believe in priorities.

The second call was from Cliff Fortana. "Will be at this number till ten-thirty. Call before then if you can."

It was now ten-twenty. Amy and I had gone to her house as planned. Only we hadn't done a whole lot of algebra. Her mom and little sister were in the kitchen making something brown and gooey, her dad was in the living room reading, and her brother was in the den watching TV. That seemed to leave only one place to study.

"We're going up to my room, Mom," Amy announced, tossing her sweater on a chair and grabbing two of the brown slices. "Algebra test tomorrow."

"Okey dokey," her mother answered cheerfully. "Don't strain anything."

I couldn't believe it! Amy was going to be in her room alone with a boy and all her mother could say was "Okey dokey!" and "Don't strain anything," whatever *that* meant. I was beginning to wonder where I'd been the past seventeen years.

"So where do you want to start?" I asked, sitting uncomfortably on the bed and looking around for some sign of her algebra text.

"Actually, I thought we might start here," Amy answered, sitting down beside me and drawing my head down to hers.

After fifteen minutes of the heaviest breathing I'd done since climbing Mount Jackson last summer I forced myself to break away and suggested that maybe we should do a little work on her algebra.

"Joe, I got a ninety-five on my final last year." She

stood up and looked down at me. "Look, I'm sorry if I came on too strong, but you are a little on the shy side, and I thought you could use some help."

I didn't have a ready answer for that, so I pulled her back down on the bed and carried on where we'd left off. I'm really quite a quick study when I finally get going.

After another half-hour of fooling around, Amy suddenly got up and began fixing her hair. I didn't know whether I'd done something wrong or failed to do something. Women are a very puzzling breed.

"What's the matter, Amy?" I asked anxiously.

"Not a thing, Joe. It's just getting a little late and I have a few things I have to do before I can go to bed."

"Oh, I see," I answered, not seeing at all. "I'll be going, then."

"No, wait a minute." She dropped her comb on the dresser and came over to stand in front of me. "The Chi Delts Harvest Dance is coming up in a couple of weeks. Paul Gross asked me to go with him, but I'd rather go with you."

"I'm not a Chi Delt, Amy," I answered. "I thought you knew that."

"I do know. I also know you've been asked to join. The initiation is before the dance, so you'd be eligible to go to it."

"I haven't decided yet if I'm going to accept their invitation."

"Oh, but you must! They're the greatest. And they have the best parties and stuff."

She looked down at me pleadingly. I was having a very hard time figuring out why a popular girl like Amy Hubank was suddenly interested in a guy like me.

As though reading my mind, she smiled and said,

"You're very special, Joe. Good-looking, a great build, and so totally uncomplicated. I like being with you, that's why I want you to join the Chi Delts. All my friends date the fraternity and I want us to be part of the fun."

"I'll think about it, Amy," I promised, "and let you know tomorrow."

"Good enough." She gave me a quick kiss, then took my hand and we walked together down to the front door.

* * *

"Cliff? This is Joe Larriby. I just got your message."

"Oh, hi, Joe. Glad you caught me. The fraternity is having a meeting and your name came up again. The guys really want to know if you're going to accept our invitation. I'm sorry to push you, but we need to know right away. Another name has been put forth for membership — someone in grade 11. Whether we take him or not depends on whether you decide to join. There's only one slot not filled."

I thought of Amy's face looking down at me and asking me to join the fraternity. If I turned them down I could pretty well forget about dating Amy again — if you could call what we had tonight a date. I knew she wasn't a snob, and I think she really liked me for myself — if that doesn't sound too conceited. But I could understand that she wanted to hang out with her girlfriends and that meant the fraternity dos.

I hesitated for just a split second as Woody's face flashed in front of my eyes, then I answered, "Yeah, sure, Cliff. I accept with pleasure."

Then I went up to bed without returning Woody's call.

Five

*H*ey, how come you didn't call me last night?"
Woody turned from his locker and watched me
open my lock.

"I'm sorry. It was pretty late when I came in."

"That's okay," he said with a grin. "Your dad said
you were at choir practice. So you decided to miss
band, eh?"

"Not exactly." I pulled a couple of books out of my
locker and stuffed my sweater on the top shelf, then
banged the door closed.

Woody pushed his glasses up on his nose and peered
at me. "What's that supposed to mean?"

"Look, Woody, I'm in kind of a hurry. We'll talk
about this later." I checked the lock and started to walk
away.

"Hey, don't you want to hear my news?" he called
after me.

"Later," I called back.

I didn't mean to be rude, but I honestly didn't want
to hear Woody going on and on about his gerbil or any
other earthshaking bulletin. Also, I didn't want to talk
about missing choir practice. I wasn't up to facing his
disapproval right then. And he would have disap-

proved. Woody Albert has to be the most honest guy I've ever met. He makes George Washington look like a compulsive liar. And I've been pretty straight myself, for that matter. I guess Woody might have understood my problem, but I don't think he would have condoned my method of handling it.

Woody and I didn't have any classes together that morning, so I didn't see him again until lunchtime. I'd spent most of the morning thinking about how I'd skipped choir and not told Dad. I've always been upfront with my parents, just the way they've always been upfront with me. I didn't like the idea of going behind their backs, but on the other hand, what choice did I have? I decided to talk it over with Woody at noon, even though I knew it wouldn't be a whole lot of fun.

But as it turned out, I didn't get a chance to talk to Woody at all.

When I went into the caf for first-period lunch, Cliff Fortana was waiting for me just inside the door. He grabbed my arm, and before I had figured out what was happening I was being steered over to the fraternity table. About ten guys were already there, and as I sat down they all rose in turn and shook my hand.

"Glad you decided to join us, Joe," Sam Quan said when this very embarrassing ritual was over.

I mumbled something that I hope sounded like "Thanks" and became very engrossed in opening my carton of milk. Naturally, I was trying to get the wrong side apart and ended up wearing half the contents, but no one seemed to notice, or at least if they did they were cool enough not to let me know. I was seriously doubting my hasty decision last night to join the frat. I don't like being in the limelight, and here I was the focus of every eye in the cafeteria. On the other hand, there was Amy. I turned to Sam and said, "Do you always greet each other like that?"

Sam laughed and passed me a handful of paper napkins. "No, of course not — only new pledges," he answered. "What are you so uptight about? Nobody's looking at you."

I made myself glance around the caf and realized he was right; no one was paying the slightest attention to our table. No one, that is, except Woody. He was sitting by himself at a table in the far corner — the one we usually sit at together — and he was watching me with an expression halfway between bewilderment and disgust.

"I hear you're playing with the Creature Comforts," one of the guys at the far end of the table called over. "They're a wicked group."

"Yeah," someone else chimed in, "Lindsay told me you landed the Halloween gig at the Elks Club."

"It's not definite yet," I answered, relieved to be able to actually contribute to the conversation. "The program guy from the Elks is looking at another group as well."

"Yeah, who?"

I told them about the Sinful Six and they all agreed that it didn't have a chance. The table then broke into small groups, and pretty soon Cliff came over and pulled up a chair beside me.

"Initiation is on Friday, Joe. Nine P.M. at Paul Gross's house. The fraternity usually meets on Tuesday but we always have our initiations on a weekend. Big party and all that. Okay for you?"

"Fine," I answered. And it would be fine too. I'd be able to make band practice and still get to Paul's in time if I left a little early.

The warning bell rang for afternoon classes and I hurried out of the caf, burying myself among my soon-to-be frat brothers. The last thing I wanted just then was to run into Woody.

As I headed for the chem lab it occurred to me that he never had told me what it was that was so urgent. Of course I hadn't really given him much of an opportunity.

* * *

I started going over to the library right after school to do my homework that week. I had a couple of reasons. First, I needed a quiet place to get my work done and our home between 3:00 and 6:00 P.M. was more like Sunday at the zoo than your normal everyday household.

Mom usually had one group of women or other from the church doing strange things with pieces of material or holding meetings in the living room; Dad watched "Gunsmoke" and "Dobie Gillis" reruns in the den; Marty practiced her clarinet in the kitchen. I guess you can see my point.

In the second place, Amy Hubank was doing a research project for history and was at the library every afternoon that week. I was kind of hoping we could do a rerun in the stacks of the night before, but Amy was all business when I suggested it. Naturally, I was totally freaked out, thinking I'd assumed something that wasn't so about us. Total confidence — that's me!

"I'm sorry, Joe, but I really have a lot of work to do," she said, only half paying attention to me. Then, spotting some guy waving at her from across the room, she muttered a hasty "See you later."

I was crushed. Had our rendezvous on her bed meant nothing to her? Did she really mean it when she said I should join the frat so we could do things together? Was it all a big joke to her?

I remembered Woody saying I was really into the big time with Amy Hubank. He was probably right. She was way out of my league.

I picked up my pen and began writing the paragraph on *The Tempest* that was due the next day. I had no trouble at all. It was exactly how I felt.

An hour or so later I was packing up my books, getting ready to go home, when Amy appeared at my elbow.

"Hi, there," she greeted me, as though nothing had happened.

"Oh, hi." I tried to sound nonchalant but it came out surly instead.

"Gee, Joe, what's the matter?"

"Nothing. Where's your *boyfriend*?"

She gave me a funny look, then started to giggle. "You mean Packy Potter? He's not my boyfriend, for gosh sakes."

"He isn't?"

"Of course not. Look, I'm sorry if I was kind of abrupt a little while ago, but it's just that I have to get this paper done, and with practice every evening this is the only time I have. Packy is a whiz at history and he's helping me. That's all."

I guess I must have still looked skeptical because she sat down beside me and took my hand. "Look, Joe, there's lots of time for us. We don't practice Saturday night, so why don't we do something then?"

I started to feel a lot better and nodded in agreement. "Great, Amy. Want to take in a movie? There's a revival of *It Happened One Night* at the Plaza." I stopped in confusion. "Maybe you don't like old movies," I offered.

"Love them. Is that the one with Clark Gable?"

"Yeah, that's it. It's one of my favorites."

"Mine too." She stood up and smiled down at me. "I've really got to get back to my paper, Joe. See you tonight at practice. And I'll be counting the hours till Saturday night."

I suppose that sounds pretty corny when you read it, but the way she said it made it sound like a Shakespeare sonnet. I was feeling so good that I was almost home before I realized I hadn't told her I'd agreed to join the fraternity.

* * *

The week went by pretty quickly, what with band practices, studying to keep up my A average (if I really do end up wanting to go to university I'll need a scholarship), and avoiding cozy little discussions about church activities with my father. Before I knew it, Friday had arrived.

Gord was good about letting me leave practice early.

"We might as well all pack it up," he said when I reminded him at eight forty-five that I had to leave. "The group has improved terrifically in the past week. I know we'll knock 'em dead at the dance."

"*If* we get the gig," Ellis muttered.

"Yeah," Mac agreed with a shrug.

Gord raised his eyebrows in mock surprise.

"Hey, didn't I mention that Bryce called this afternoon?"

Dead silence as four pairs of eyes turned to him.

"So?" Amy's voice was low and shaky.

"So we got the job."

Four pairs of hands descended on his throat.

"Hey, wait a minute!" Gord laughed as he tried to disentangle himself. "I didn't tell you before because I wanted this to be a good rehearsal. You'd have all freaked out if you'd known ahead of time."

"Gord, people have had their lips torn off for less than that," Amy cried. "How could you leave us in suspense?"

"Was there ever any doubt that we'd get the job?"

"Yes!" Amy yelled. Then she settled back and grinned. "This calls for a celebration."

"Let's go for burgers," Mac suggested.

Everyone nodded in agreement and began arguing about where the best burgers were made.

I picked up my guitar and started to go upstairs.

"Hey, aren't you coming with us, Joe?" Ellis called.

"Can't," I called back. "I've gotta go to a meeting." I got to the top of the stairs and started down the hall.

"Yeah," I heard Gord say, "Joe's been asked to join the Chi Delts. Initiation tonight."

"Really?" Mac replied. "Big time, eh?"

I could almost see Ellis shrug.

More than anything I wanted to say to hell with the fraternity and go off with the band. But I'd made a commitment and I always kept my word. At least I did then.

A moment later Amy came rushing upstairs.

"Is it true, Joe? Did you really decide to join the frat?"

"Yeah, I guess so."

"That's great! Then we'll be able to go to the Harvest Dance?"

So she really did mean everything she said. She

wanted me to take her to the dance. Maybe she even wanted us to go steady. I wondered if I would ever understand women.

"Guess so." I grinned. "But unless I get moving very fast I won't make the initiation." I gave her a hasty wave and left the house. I had a little less than ten minutes to get to Paul Gross's house.

Six

Mrs. Gross answered the door and led me into the living room. Two other guys were already there, sitting on the couch, one of them looking as nervous as I felt, the other smoking a cigarette and smiling as though he owned the world.

Mrs. Gross left us with a cheerful "The boys are downstairs. They should be up to get you in a few minutes."

I sat down on a chair opposite the couch and nodded to the other two. The nervous one stood up and took a couple of steps toward me.

"I'm Aaron Gold and this is Dewie Riceman," he said, sticking out his hand. "We're in grade 11."

I stood up and took his hand, feeling a little foolish.

"Hi, I'm Joe Larriby. Twelve."

"Yeah, I know." Aaron nodded. "You're a friend of Woody Albert's, aren't you? He's in my chess club."

"Yeah, Woody and I have been friends for a long time. He's a great guy." I started feeling a little more comfortable and began talking about some of the crazy things Woody and I used to do.

"How come you waited till grade 12 to join the frat?"

the other guy interrupted from the couch where he had stayed seated.

"I hadn't been asked," I answered, the comfortable feeling quickly replaced by annoyance.

"Is that a fact? I was asked to join the first week of high school."

"Well, good for you!" The guy was beginning to get to me. If he was going to be my fraternity brother, I wondered if I wasn't making a big mistake being here at all.

"Well, I suppose they can only take people when there are openings." Aaron hastened to calm the storm that was beginning to gather between us.

Before any more harsh words were said, Cliff appeared in the doorway.

"Okay, we're ready for you. The guys are waiting downstairs. We'll take you one at a time starting with — " he paused dramatically " — Aaron." He turned and walked back down the hall.

Aaron grinned and rushed after him, leaving me and Huey or Louie or whatever his name was to entertain each other. We sat and glared at each other for a couple of minutes, then I decided that if we were going to be in the same fraternity I ought to make a pass at getting along with him.

Keeping up a conversation, however, was tough sledding. The guy was either trying to hide his nervousness by being supercool (read *rude* or *sarcastic*) or else he was a genuine scuzball. He made tasteless jokes about the church, put down the Creature Comforts — he'd seen Motley Crüe in person three years ago and considered himself an expert on rock — ran down every teacher in the school, then hinted that he was doing the Chi Delts a big favor in accepting their invitation to join them. Obviously, getting along with him was going to be next to impossible.

I tuned him out after the first seven or eight put-downs and began to think about Amy and our date the next night. I wondered if I should suggest we go up to Scotchman's Hill, the make-out spot, after the movie. If I did, maybe she'd be offended. On the other hand, if I didn't, she might think I was a total wimp.

About half an hour passed before Cliff came upstairs and took God's gift to the Chi Delts downstairs, leaving me alone to wonder for the millionth time if I was doing the right thing by joining the frat. The guys in the band obviously didn't think too much of it, judging from Mac's comment. Or maybe they were just envious.

I guess maybe the frat guys figured out I might just be thinking along those lines, so they sent Sam Quan up to prevent me from bolting.

"What's going on down there anyway?" I asked when he'd sat down and explained that he was going to keep me company until it was my turn.

"It's the initiation rites," he answered. "Each pledge has to be initiated alone. It's no big deal, really — just a lot of ritual, learning the handshake, the secret code words — you'll see."

"It takes quite a while, doesn't it?"

"Well, see, it's not just the ceremony. Before the pledge is accepted as a full member of the fraternity he has to prove himself to be worthy of joining the brotherhood. Each new member is given a task he has to complete before he takes his final vows."

"Geez, it sounds like the priesthood!"

"Hardly!" Sam gave me a strange look and kind of grinned to himself.

I was soon to learn why.

I won't bore you with a blow-by-blow description of the initiation ritual. It was kind of silly but it had its moments. When all the guys pledged to stand by me no matter what and to consider my friendship a sacred trust, I got a little choked up. For the first time in my life I felt I was really part of a close group instead of being an outsider with only one real friend.

Then came the initiation stunt they had assigned me. I think they must have spent hours working on the idea. How else could they have come up with something that would be sure to test my loyalty to the hilt?

* * *

The party that followed the initiation was really pretty tame.

"We're saving the real celebration for the Harvest Dance," Cliff explained as we sat together drinking beer and sharing a pizza. "You're coming, aren't you?"

"I guess so," I answered, a little uncertain whether Amy would still want to go with me. She had me so confused with her hot and cold behavior that I didn't know what to expect.

"You want us to get you a date?"

"No, I think I'm taking Amy Hubank."

Cliff's eyebrows rose at this announcement. "I thought she was going with Paul Gross."

"Yeah, she did mention that he'd asked her, but she turned him down."

"I see." He took a gulp of beer and stared into space. A minute or so went by, and I wondered what I'd done now. Then he spoke. "In this fraternity we don't compete with our brothers," he told me. "Of course, you didn't know that at the time, so we'll let this one go, but in the future, Joe, remember when a brother asks a girl for a date, another brother doesn't try to beat his time."

"But I didn't — " I protested.

Cliff cut me short. "I know you didn't. And I know it won't happen again." He gave me a big grin that took the sting out of his words and stood up. "I've got to get up early tomorrow — my job starts at eight — so I think I'll be heading home. Can I give you a lift, Joe?"

"No thanks. I only live a couple of blocks away. I'll walk." The truth is I wanted a little time for myself. I needed to do a lot of thinking.

* * *

I'm supposed to work from nine till five on Saturdays, but there was no way I could miss practice, so when I got to work a little before nine I went over and spoke to Mr. Granger.

"I'm afraid I'm going to have to leave at two o'clock today," I told him. "I'll try to get all the deliveries done by then."

"Oh, Joe, that's not good." Mr. Granger turned from the side of beef he was cutting up and put down his cleaver. "What am I going to do about the orders that come in after two?"

"Well, maybe I could find someone to take over for me," I offered. Woody didn't work on Saturdays except around his house. His dad and mom wanted him to "enjoy his youth," as they put it, and were dead set against his getting a job. Ordinarily he'd have been more than willing to help me out; he'd done it a few times before. However, I wasn't sure how he'd react to my asking him. The truth is, I'd hardly spoken to him during the past week. I'd eaten lunch at the fraternity table every day — not because I wanted to that much, but Cliff insisted. And my evenings were taken up with band practice, of course. I tried to talk to him a couple of times during class changes, but he wasn't too receptive.

"Very well," Mr. Granger muttered, "but I'm not too happy with this arrangement. I trust it won't be a recurring problem."

I assured him that it wouldn't, knowing that if I stayed with the band I'd probably have to take every Saturday afternoon off. But I'd worry about that when the time came.

I went to the back and called Woody from Mr. Granger's office. I didn't want anyone hearing me if I had to do any pleading. It was just as well I'd taken the precaution.

"Woody, it's me," I began, trying to sound a lot more confident than I felt. "How're you doing?"

"Okay." Period.

"Ah, look, I'm sorry I haven't called you, but it's been a crazy week."

"So I understand. We missed you at Doodles last night."

Omigod! I'd forgotten all about it. Doodles, in case you're wondering what anything so cutesy could possibly refer to, is the name the moms and kids at the Women's Shelter gave to us. A few of us high school students go there every Friday night to entertain them. The women are there with their children because their husbands beat them so much that they had to get away from home. The clientele changes pretty frequently since they can only stay for six weeks, and the waiting list to get in is awesome. It really makes me wonder about my own sex.

Anyway, I play the guitar, a couple of girls from

beauty culture teach hairstyling and makeup, another guy tells stories and Woody does mime. The kids love him. It's funny about Woody; he's so shy around people ordinarily, but as soon as he gets his white face on, he just blossoms. We've been going to the shelter for about a year now, and it's about the neatest thing I've ever done. I can't believe I forgot about it last night.

"Woody, I'm really sorry. Something came up and I forgot to phone and let them know I wouldn't be able to make it."

"Yeah, I know, Joe. Frat initiation."

This conversation *wasn't* going the way I'd hoped. I remembered the last time Woody called me and said he had something urgent to tell me. This seemed as good a time as any to ask him about it.

"So what was the urgent message you had for me?" As soon as the words were out I wanted to tear out my throat. What a sleazy thing to do!

"Oh, you remembered, eh? It wasn't anything much — nothing like pledging the frat."

I didn't even try for a comeback. I deserved anything he wanted to throw at me. "So what was it?"

"Channel 10 asked me to do a weekly stint on the children's hour. I'm on from five-fifteen till five-thirty every Thursday."

"Woody, that's excellent! Why didn't you tell me before this?"

"I tried to."

I was beginning to wonder if there was anything more he could come up with to complete my total destruction when I remembered why I'd called.

"When do you start?" I asked, trying to figure out how to broach the subject of his filling in for me at the store.

"We tape next Wednesday. It'll be run the next day."
He was starting to sound a little warmer.

"Great. I'll be watching — in fact, the whole family
will be glued to the TV set."

"Thanks, Joe. Say, maybe you'd like to come down
to the studio with me?"

"Sure, I'd love it."

"Did you have something on your mind when you
called? I thought you'd be at work by now."

"I am. Actually, I was hoping you could fill in for me
this aft. About two o'clock. I have band practice," I
quickly explained, before he thought I might be doing
something with the fraternity.

"Sure, okay, Joe. As long as it's all right with Mr.
Granger. He wasn't too happy with me the last time I
filled in for you, if you remember."

I remembered. Woody had managed to get his pant
leg caught in his bike chain and fall off right in front
of old Mrs. Peterson's house. Her semivicious bulldog
bit him on the arm then took off with about ten pounds
of top sirloin. He couldn't finish his deliveries, and Mr.
Granger had to go over to Mrs. Peterson's house and
pick up what was left of the stuff and deliver it
himself — after he took Woody to emergency to have
his arm bandaged.

"Mr. Granger's probably forgotten all about it," I
assured him. "Anyway, if you could get here about one
forty-five I'd appreciate it."

"I'll be there. And maybe we could do something
together tonight, eh?"

That was it! He'd done it! Total guilt trip.

"Geez, I'm sorry, Woody, but I've got a date. But
how about tomorrow? We could go to the science

museum — there's a new star show on — and maybe
you could stay overnight."

"A date? With a girl?"

"That's the usual drill. It's Amy Hubank, in case you
were wondering."

"Wow!" Pause. "Well, have fun." He sounded as if
he'd been told the sun wouldn't be coming up anymore.
"I'll see you this afternoon." Then he hung up.

I went back into the store and told Mr. Granger that
I had a replacement coming in at two. I didn't mention
that it was Woody. No point in all of us being depressed.

I picked up my first orders and took them out to the
station wagon. It wasn't until I was at my third house
that I forgot about Woody and began to think about my
date that night with Amy.

Then I remembered the initiation stunt I had to do
and I started to feel a little sick.

Seven

I wondered if Amy would remember that we'd planned on going to a movie that night. I hadn't really talked to her since the day in the library. So when I got to practice a little after two, I wasn't quite sure what to say to her. I didn't need to worry, though. She said it first.

"Can you pick me up about six forty-five, Joe?" she asked as we were getting our equipment out. "I checked and the first show starts at seven-fifteen. I hate going to the second show; it makes it too late to do much."

I nodded in my usual suave, sophisticated way and blushed. The guys were all watching us with great interest. Mac shrugged at Ellis.

* * *

Needless to say, I had a wonderful time. And I think Amy did too. The movie was as great as I remembered it; the last booth at Bernie's Burgers was (unbelievably) empty, so we were able to talk in private, which we did for about two hours. Before taking her home I drove up to Scotchman's Hill and parked overlooking the ravine. The night was clear, so the view of the city was fabulous. It seemed perfectly natural to put my arm around her and have her rest her head on my shoulder.

"It's so romantic up here, Joe." She sighed. "Did you ever hear about the couple who made the suicide pact and jumped into the ravine together?"

To be honest, I didn't think that was the most romantic thing I could think of, but I didn't tell Amy that. "What happened?" I asked instead.

"It was a long time ago — before my mom and dad were born. Grandma used to tell the story. It seems this girl from one of the rich families in town fell in love with a young man who worked in her father's store. Her parents found out about it and were going to send her away to live with relatives in England until she got over him. It was all very Victorian. Anyway, she arranged to meet him up here the night before she was to leave, and they threw themselves off the edge of the cliff. When they found the bodies, they were still holding hands." Amy sighed contentedly and snuggled closer.

"Is that really true?" I asked, appalled at the thought that anyone would willingly take his own life. It was such a stupid waste. If they *had* gotten married they probably would have ended up with six kids and middle-age spread. Not my idea of something you threw yourself over a cliff for.

"Oh, yes!" Amy answered. "Wouldn't it be wonderful to love someone so much that you literally couldn't live without him?"

I decided it was time to cut the gruesome talk and get a little action going, so I turned her head toward me and bent over to kiss her.

We spent another two hours looking at the view and in between glances we managed to get very friendly.

Now don't get me wrong; we didn't do anything I'd be ashamed to tell Mom — Dad, maybe, but not Mom. It was even better than in Amy's bedroom, I guess because I was a little more experienced and I wasn't terrified that someone would walk in on us.

I took her home about one and drove the rest of the way in a total fog. In fact, I was so out of it that I didn't think about the initiation stunt I had to do until Mom called me the next morning to get ready for church.

* * *

If our choir wore robes like most other church choirs, the frat would have had to think of something else for me to do for initiation. But a couple of years ago the board voted to get rid of them and go to black pants/skirts and white shirts/blouses. They figured it was more modern. I would have been a lot happier if they'd modernized some of their musty groups instead. So there I was in the choir room waiting for the opening hymn and wanting to throw up. I didn't know how I was going to do it, but I knew I had to. Somebody from the fraternity would be in the congregation checking up on me.

As the notes of the organ began and the procession started down the aisle to the choir loft, I closed my eyes and prayed for a miracle: everyone in the church would suddenly be smitten by temporary blindness.

When we took our places in the choir loft, still standing, I checked out the congregation for frat brothers. I wasn't disappointed. The whole fraternity was sitting in the third and fourth pews on my left. The hymn was over. I sat down and laid my hymn book on my lap. Dad took his place behind the pulpit and began his first prayer. Then came the second hymn, the announcements, the reading from the Old Testament, then the solo.

Me.

I hadn't been to choir practice, of course, but Dunn the Hun always had the music for the services organized a month ahead. The anthem and soloist were even printed in the church bulletin along with Dad's sermon topics. I'd known for a couple of weeks that I'd be singing a solo of "How Great Thou Art." So had the fraternity.

I stood up and moved from my place in the back of the choir loft up to the front of the altar. The organist played the first few notes of the introduction and I began to sing. Then the tittering started. Quietly at first, then louder. Someone guffawed. I caught Dad looking over at me from his chair on the other side of the altar and gasping. I kept on singing, keeping my eyes on my music and not daring to look at anyone.

By the time I'd finished the last verse of the anthem everyone in the church was laughing. Everyone except the people in the choir. They were behind me. However, when I turned around to go back to my seat Saralee Tidbell, who was sitting in the first row of the stalls, took one look and covered her eyes. The rest of the choir started to laugh. I sat down and did up my zipper.

* * *

"I don't know how you could possibly have disgraced yourself that way, Joseph. Surely you must have realized something was wrong." Dad was attacking the chicken as if he was wishing it were me sitting on the platter.

"I was so embarrassed I wanted to just fall through

the floor down into the Sunday school room," Marty growled. "And you know how I hate Sunday school."

"I'm sure Joe didn't do it on purpose, for heaven's sake," Mom put in. "Now, let's just forget about it and enjoy our dinner."

I guess I could have let it go at that, but I didn't feel right about having them think I didn't know what I was doing.

"Actually, Mom, I *did* do it on purpose. It was part of my initiation into the fraternity."

"What!" Dad stabbed the chicken. "Are you saying you deliberately disgraced yourself — and the rest of your family as well?"

"I had to. If I'd refused to do it, the fraternity wouldn't have taken me."

"Well, I never!" Dad laid his carving knife down on the platter and sat back in his chair. "I am very disappointed in you, Joseph: making a mockery of the holy service, and for what? To join a foolish group of young men who have nothing better to do than invent sacrilegious stunts. I knew nothing good would come of you leaving Young People's to join that wild bunch of musicians."

I felt myself slowly getting angrier and angrier as he went on about my new friends and how they were corrupting me. He had no right to judge them. He'd never even met them, for pete's sake! And as far as the initiation stunt went, I was the one who had to take the guff, not him.

"Damn it all anyway," I cried, jumping up from my seat. "It's not such a big deal. Sure, it was a crazy stunt, but it didn't hurt anyone. And as for my friends, they're one helluva lot more fun than those holier-than-thou hypocrites in Young People's."

Dad's face dropped about a foot. Marty and Mom were staring at me openmouthed. Never in my almost eighteen years had I spoken to my father like that. I felt the anger drain away as I watched his expression turn from furious surprise to sad resignation.

"I'm sorry," I muttered. "I didn't mean to hurt you, but you've got to understand. I have new friends, new interests, and it hurts me too when you put them down. I'm sorry too about the fiasco at church. I didn't want to do it; I've been dreading it for days. But don't you see? I *had* to do it."

"If you say so, Joseph. I apologize for criticizing your friends. I'm sure you know what you're doing." He picked up the carving tools and started back on the chicken. He looked totally defeated.

"Now, sit down, Joe, and have your dinner," Mom urged with fake cheerfulness.

"I'm not hungry. May I please be excused? I'm going to be late for practice."

Mom nodded mutely. Dad continued to carve the chicken. He didn't look up as I left the room.

* * *

After practice Amy asked me to come over to her house. We finished at three-thirty and I was supposed to meet Woody at four. We were going to take in the star show, then grab a hamburger before evening services at the church. I wanted more than anything to go with Amy, but a promise is a promise.

"Gee, I'm sorry, I can't," I apologized. "I promised someone I'd go to the science museum with him."

"Okay." Amy smiled, not looking nearly as crushed as I'd hoped she would. "Maybe some other time."

I took a deep breath and plunged in. "How about this

evening? That is, unless you have something else planned."

Her smile turned into a knowing grin. "Are you sure you don't have any *meetings* this evening?"

I blushed and shook my head. "Nope."

"Okay, then. Come on over about seven-thirty."

It wasn't till Woody and I were sitting in the drive-in waiting for the carhop to bring our burgers that I remembered that I'd asked him to stay the night.

"Gee, this has been fun, Joe. Just like old times," Woody said. He was grinning his shy grin and pulling at his right ear the way he does when he's embarrassed. "I'll stop by at the house and pick up my books so I can go directly to school from your place tomorrow morning."

"Oh, yeah," I mumbled and turned quickly away to roll down the window. The girl came a moment later with our food, and I made a big production of getting the tray hooked onto the window and paying her while I stalled for time. When I turned back to Woody he was still grinning that happy-sappy grin. I knew I couldn't disappoint him.

I didn't say anything about my date with Amy. I'd cancel when we got home. Instead, I asked him to tell me all about his TV spot.

"I'm really excited about it, Joe." He began biting into his burger and splattering food all over in his eagerness. "I realize it's no big deal — just a local show nobody watches — but the experience I'll get will be invaluable."

"Yeah, I suppose it will. Are you thinking of making a career out of acting?"

"Who knows? Dad and Mom want me to go into something traditional like medicine, but I love mime so much. When I'm doing my act I forget I'm dull, funny-looking Woody Albert and feel really good about myself."

I just nodded. How do you answer that?

* * *

We got back to the house about six-thirty and I made an excuse to go upstairs so I could use the phone in Mom and Dad's bedroom. Amy answered on the second ring.

"Hi, it's Joe."

"Yes, I know. I recognized your voice."

"Amy, I'm really sorry but I won't be able to come over this evening. Something's come up."

There was a slight pause, then she answered. "I see. The *meeting* is on after all, eh?" There was a touch of amused condescension in her voice.

"No, nothing like that!" I cried. "It's just that I promised someone I'd do something and I forgot about it."

"Sure, Joe. That's okay. Maybe another time." The amusement had turned to anger. I knew I had to stop her before she hung up and probably never spoke to me again.

"Look, Amy. About the Harvest Dance. It's next Saturday night."

"So?"

"Well, I was sort of hoping you'd go with me. Remember, we talked about it at your place last Tuesday."

"I remember."

I started to get really anxious. She wasn't giving me much help. Maybe she'd changed her mind and was going with Paul Gross after all. Boy, if I'd gone through all that business with the fraternity for nothing . . .

"Well? Will you?"

"If you're sure you won't have to suddenly cancel at the last minute because of something your daddy says you have to do."

It was a low blow and not worthy of her, I thought.

"Never mind, then. Forget it."

Suddenly she was back to normal. "Oh, Joe, I'm sorry. Of course I want to go to the dance with you. But I get so angry when you turn me down because of something at the church. It's not that I don't like going to church — I still go to Sunday morning services — but I'm not wedded to it like you seem to be."

"It's different for me, Amy. My father's the minister. But I know what you mean and I'm getting out of a lot of the church activities. I've quit Young People's and I've given up evening services. I'll probably quit the choir too. Tonight has nothing to do with the church. If you really want to know, I asked Woody Albert to stay overnight and I forgot about it when I said I'd come over to your place."

"Well, if that's all, bring him over. I'll fix him up with one of my friends."

"Hey, that's great," I replied, relief flooding over me. "We'll be there in half an hour."

Suddenly, everything was falling into place in my life. If Woody and Amy's friend clicked, we could double-date. I might even be able to get him into the fraternity. After all, Aaron already knew him. I promised myself I'd make it up to Dad for the fight we had at dinner and I'd find some way to get to choir practice on Tuesday. No more going behind his back.

That's what I told myself, but it didn't work out quite the way I'd planned.

Eight

A s we were driving over to Amy's house I asked Woody how it had gone yesterday afternoon. I'd avoided the subject up till then, afraid of what he might tell me.

He looked crestfallen. "I thought Mr. Granger might have talked to you already," he mumbled, pulling at his ear.

"About what?" I held my breath.

"About the pumpkins," he answered.

"The pumpkins?"

"Uh-huh. It wasn't really my fault, Joe. The back door on the van doesn't shut properly."

I drove to the side of the road and stopped. "Okay, give it to me straight."

"Well, it all started when Mr. Granger told me I had to deliver a load of pumpkins to Our Lady's over on the other side of town. Seems the women were making pumpkin pies to sell at the church today. He let me take the van and I was feeling pretty good about it. Anyway, I was tooling along Grant Boulevard when I heard a kind of bump behind me. I didn't pay too much attention; I figured I'd hit a pothole. Then I heard another bump, then another. Then there was this horrible screech of brakes and a deafening crash. I figured maybe I'd better check so I pulled over to the side and got out of the van." He stopped and took a deep breath.

"And?"

"And the street behind me was covered with smashed pumpkins. A car following me had skidded in the pumpkin pulp and had run into a truck coming in the opposite direction. Another car coming up from behind couldn't stop and piled into the first car and the truck. Do you want me to go on? It gets worse."

"Oh, geez, Woody! Was anyone hurt?"

"No, but they were sure mad. The guy from the truck slipped when he climbed out to see what had happened and ended up covered from head to toe with pumpkin pulp. The guy from the first car laughed and the trucker picked up a busted pumpkin and dumped it on his head. A couple more cars had crashed into the pile-up and pretty soon everyone was throwing squashed pumpkins at everyone else. By the time the police got there, about seven cars had piled up and a dozen or so people were covered with pumpkin pulp. It looked like a scene from a horror movie, *The Squash That Ate New York*." He giggled feebly and looked out the window.

"What happened then?"

"The police took everyone's name and called Mr. Granger. He arrived about ten minutes later."

I cringed, not wanting to hear the answer but knowing I'd have to ask. "What did he say?"

"Actually, he didn't say anything for quite a while. He didn't seem to be able to speak. The police charged him with public nuisance or something, then let us go. He got in his car and motioned for me to follow him back to the store in the van. When we got there, all he said was 'Don't ever let me see you near this store again. And that goes for your unreliable friend too.' Then he went inside and slammed the door. I didn't know what else to do, so I went home."

I didn't say anything for a minute while my scrambled brain tried to process his incredible story. Mr. Granger was charged with something and would probably have to pay a fine and damages; I was responsible for the accident, indirectly anyway, therefore I should have to pay instead of Mr. Granger; I no longer had a job, therefore I had no money to pay for the accident. It was very depressing. I banged my hand on the steering wheel a couple of times and swore under my breath. Woody shuddered beside me.

Then I started to visualize the whole crazy mess and I started to laugh. I leaned over the steering wheel and laughed till my stomach hurt. Woody just sat there saying nothing and looking scared. That made me laugh harder. Finally, I got control and wiped my eyes.

"It's okay, Woody. I didn't want the job anyway. Besides, I need to be able to practice with the band Saturday afternoons."

"Then you're not mad at me?"

"Naw. The only thing is I'll have to find a way to pay Mr. Granger for the damages."

"Don't worry about that, Joe." Woody grinned, obviously delighted to be able to make amends. "I've got lots of money saved up. I'll take care of it; after all, it *was* my fault."

"We'll talk about it," I answered and started up the car. "Now let's forget about it and plan on having a blast tonight."

Woody nodded and looked scared again. I knew this time it didn't have anything to do with pumpkins. This was Woody's first date, and I figured he was probably terrified.

* * *

Amy met us at the door and took us directly downstairs to the family room.

"Mom and Dad are in New York for the weekend," she announced, "so we have the place to ourselves."

Woody's date, a tiny little blond girl I'd seen around school but didn't know, was already there, sitting in a very large recliner. She looked about twelve years old.

"This is Cookie." Amy smiled, gesturing to the girl. "And, Cookie, this is Joe and . . . ?" She looked inquiringly at Woody, and I realized I hadn't bothered to introduce him to Amy when we came in. Smooth move!

"Woody," I finished quickly.

The blonde giggled. "Did you bring your clarinet?"

Woody looked baffled.

"Not Woody Allen." I laughed, trying to cut a little of the tension that was building up. "Woody Albert. And he plays Galaga, not the clarinet."

"Oh, really?" The blonde clapped her hands and giggled again. "I just *love* that game. Are you any good?"

Woody dropped his eyes and blushed. "Not bad."

"Oh, I just bet you're great." She moved over in the recliner and said, "Come over and sit by me and we'll compare high scores."

I decided she was either a lot older than twelve or very precocious. Woody shuffled over to Cookie's chair and Amy put a tape on the stereo.

"Come on, Joe, let's dance."

I watched Woody as he perched uncomfortably on

the arm of the recliner. I should never have brought him here, I thought. He's not ready for the Cookies of this world. Then I started to dance with Amy — very close — and Woody's problem faded very quickly.

"Who wants some wine?" Amy asked when the tape finished.

Cookie jumped up and cried, "I do! I do!" like the kid in the sugarless-gum ad.

Amy went behind the bar, brought out a bottle of sherry and three glasses, and put them on the coffee table in front of Cookie.

"None for me," I protested when Cookie began pouring very generous slugs into the glasses.

"Me either," Amy said.

Cookie shrugged and muttered, "All the more for us, eh, Woody Albert?"

Amy put another tape on the stereo and we began dancing again. When the tape finished, she turned the lights off and led me to the couch across the room. I won't bore you with the details of the next hour or so. Just take my word that it was a very moving experience.

When we turned the lights back on, I looked over to see how Woody and his confection were getting on. He and Cookie were sitting together in the recliner. Woody was staring into space with a goofy expression on his face. Cookie looked annoyed.

"Hey, are you okay?" I asked.

His eyeballs disappeared into the back of his head and he burped delicately.

"Yeah, I'm great. Just great. A little hungry, though."

Amy looked at Woody, then at me.

"I'd better make a pot of coffee and get some food into him. Come on, Joe, and give me a hand."

We went upstairs and Amy got busy with the coffee grinder while I dug into the fridge for bread and stuff to make sandwiches. While we waited for the coffee to perk we wandered into the living room and did an instant replay of our action downstairs. I was getting pretty accomplished, if I do say so myself.

We were interrupted a few minutes later by Cookie's shrill voice demanding we get our butts downstairs on the double.

Amy looked at me and shrugged. I got up and followed her out of the room.

When we arrived downstairs we found Woody lying on the floor with his eyes closed and Cookie tapping her foot, looking very angry.

"What happened?" I asked, staring down at Woody.

"Are you blind or something?" Cookie spat out. "He passed out. God, I hate a guy who can't hold his liquor!"

I looked over at the table and saw the sherry bottle was nearly empty. Poor Woody. I didn't think he'd ever had more than one bottle of beer at a time in his whole life.

I managed to wake him up and get him over to the chair where he promptly tossed his cookies all over his Cookie.

Anger turned to fury and Cookie screamed, "Get that horrible little man out of here!" and ran for the bathroom. Woody collapsed on the chair, and Amy and I cleaned up the mess. Then Amy went upstairs and brought down the coffeepot and plate of sandwiches. We tried to get some coffee and food into Woody, but it was a hopeless task.

Amy sighed. "I'm sorry, Joe, I should never have brought out the wine. I thought it might loosen him up a little."

"It did that," I answered with a groan. "I guess I'd better get him home."

Somehow between us Amy and I got Woody up the stairs and into my car. Cookie stayed locked in the bathroom. Now, my only problem was to get him into the house without my parents seeing him.

Nine

Woody fell asleep again while we were driving home. I had one wild time waking him up enough to get him into the house. I had to half carry him along the walk and drag him up the steps. No lights were on except for the one lamp in the living room that Mom always leaves lit. I figured I had it made as I opened the door and eased Woody into the hall.

Halfway up the stairs he started to slip and I paused to shift him higher up under my arm. He woke up and grinned at me.

"Hey, Joe, how're ya doing?" he yelled.

"Shut up, for pete's sake. You'll wake the whole family." I shifted him again and started to climb the rest of the stairs.

We were a couple of steps from the top when he let out a wild laugh and yelled, "Chocolate chippie Cookie! Coconutty Cookie!" I put my hand up to cover his mouth and lost my grip on his slumping body. Before I knew what had happened he slipped from my arm and went rolling down the stairs.

As I rushed down after him I heard the door to Mom and Dad's bedroom open and Dad's voice calling, "Who's there? What's going on?"

I didn't know what to expect when I reached Woody's body lying on the floor at the bottom of the flight of stairs. He'd bounced down about fifteen steps and he could easily have broken every bone in his body or even be . . . I didn't want to even think of that. However, when I bent over him he raised his head and giggled. "What're you doin' up there, Joe?"

I leaned back, weak with relief as Woody sat up, saw my father and mother standing at the head of the stairs, and waved. "Hi, Mr. and Mrs. Larriby. Nice night, isn't it?" He giggled again and passed out.

Dad and I got Woody up the stairs and onto my bed. Mom came in and kind of cleaned him up where he'd upchucked on himself, then Dad and I undressed him and got him under the covers.

"You'd better sleep on the daybed in the den, dear," Mom said as we closed the bedroom door. Then with a pointed look at Dad she continued, "We'll talk about this in the morning."

Needless to say I didn't have the best night's sleep of my life.

* * *

I got up as soon as I heard Mom in the kitchen. I figured it would be better to talk to her first before Dad heard my story. She's always been a great buffer between us, and today I needed her as never before.

She turned off the burner under the bacon when I came in the room, poured herself a cup of coffee, and sat down. I got a glass of milk and sat across from her. "Okay, what happened?" She took of sip of coffee and looked at me.

"Woody got into the sherry at Amy's house. I think he must have drunk nearly the whole bottle."

"That was fairly obvious. The question is why did he do it and why did you let him?"

"Well, see, there was this girl — a friend of Amy's. I guess Woody was scared of her and figured a little Dutch courage wouldn't hurt. He overdid it."

"Didn't he just? And I repeat: why did you let him?"

"I didn't know he was drinking so much."

"Couldn't you see what he was doing? I assume you were all in the same room."

"The lights were out."

"Oh." She paused. "That explains a good deal. Were you drinking too, Joe?"

"No. Neither was Amy."

"I see. Well, the problem is, what are we going to tell your father? You know how he abhors liquor, even wine. The fact that you were at a party where liquor was served will not sit well with him."

"Yeah, I know. What do you think I should tell him?"

"I suggest the truth." Dad was standing in the doorway glaring at me. "Now, young man, I want an explanation for last night's outrageous performance."

"It was all a big mistake," I began. "Woody's not used to drinking and he got a little too much sherry."

"A little too much? He smelled like a distillery! And what was he doing drinking in the first place?"

I tried to explain how Woody was nervous about being with a girl, but I might as well have been talking to the stove. When I'd finished, he stared at me for at least two minutes without saying anything. Then he spoke.

"I don't know what's happening to you, Joe. You're turning your back on everything you once believed in. First you abandon Young People's when they need you as a leader, then you get involved in this rock band doing goodness knows what. Now you're attending drinking parties."

"It wasn't a drinking party!" I retorted, my anger at his narrowminded attitude overcoming my natural reluctance to crossing him. "Amy brought out a bottle of sherry, that's all."

My argument might have had a lot more effect if Woody hadn't chosen that moment to stagger into the kitchen.

Dad took one look at him and muttered, "I rest my case."

Mom didn't say a word as she poured Woody a glass of orange juice and handed him a couple of aspirins.

He looked like a cross between a drug addict gone cold turkey and a mugging victim. His eyes were bloodshot, outlined with heavy dark circles, and his whole body — what you could see of it — was black and blue.

"Would someone mind telling me what happened to me last night?" he asked after he'd downed the orange juice in one swig. "My head is awfully sore and I seem to be a bit bruised."

The understatement of the century.

"Don't you remember anything, Woody?" I asked.

"I seem to remember a girl called Candy or Toffee or something. She was very aggressive."

I started to laugh and Mom gave me a warning look. Dad sat down at the table and glared at me. No one said anything and Woody continued to look baffled and beaten — literally.

A couple of minutes later Marty came into the kitchen. She took one look at Woody and exclaimed, "Gory! What happened to you? Did the Mafia find out you were dealing bubble gum in their territory?"

You might have gathered Marty watches far too much TV.

"It's no concern of yours, Mary Martha," Dad answered sharply. "Sit down and eat your breakfast."

None of us had ever heard Dad raise his voice to Marty before. To anyone, for that matter. Woody gave me a questioning look and I shook my head. This was no time to discuss the events of the previous night.

Somehow I managed to eat a full breakfast. Nothing short of nuclear devastation can curb my appetite, it seems. As a matter of fact, when I'm nervous I get even hungrier, and I sure was nervous right then.

After a decade or so Dad put his napkin down and, turning to me, said, "I'd like to speak to you alone in the den," and left the room. I reluctantly followed.

We sat down on chairs facing each other and Dad made a pyramid of his fingertips, staring at me and not saying anything for what seemed like about three hours. When he finally spoke, his voice was low and controlled.

"I shall, of course, have to speak to Mr. and Mrs. Hubank. They are good church people, and I'm sure they are unaware that their daughter is serving liquor to her friends during their absence."

"Oh, no, Dad. Amy didn't mean any harm. How could she possibly think Woody would get carried away and drink himself silly?"

"Nevertheless, that's what I intend to do. As for Woody, he can explain his actions to his parents himself. It is of no concern to me."

He paused and looked down at his hands.

I waited, wondering if he could possibly be finished with me. No such luck.

"You, however, are a different matter," he continued.

"I care very much what happens to you, Joseph. What occurred last night will never occur again. Do you understand?"

I nodded. "Sure, Dad, it won't. I promise."

"I believe you are associating with the wrong kind of people — people who will harm you in the long run."

I began to protest and he put up his hand to stop me.

"I know. You tell me they are your friends, but they are exerting an adverse influence on you. I cannot order you to change your friendships — that is your own personal decision — but I would be very much relieved if you would break off your associations with that band and the fraternity with its irreverent initiation ceremonies. They are not the sort of companions suitable for the son of a minister."

"I can't desert the band!" I responded. "They're depending on me. And the fraternity guys are great, no matter what you think. Sure, that initiation stunt was stupid, but they didn't do it to make fun of the church." I was getting a little steamed. Next he'd be asking me to give up Amy, the booze pusher.

"As you wish. That is your decision, and much as it pains me, I shall respect it. However, I am still the head of this household, and as long as you continue to live here, you will conform to house rules. As of tonight you will be home by ten o'clock for the next two weeks. Do I make myself clear?"

"As crystal," I sighed. Dad is really a very intelligent man, but sometimes I wonder if he has any idea what's going on in the world around him. Honestly, I think he still believes that grass is something you mow and a girl shouldn't let a guy kiss her unless they're engaged.

I knew there was no point arguing with him about the curfew; his mind was made up. And if it was so important to him for me to quit the frat and the band, I'd have to very carefully think out what I would do. I had to find some way to keep him happy without breaking with the two things that were making my life so great. I'd come a long way in the past few months. I was no longer Holy Joe the goody-goody preacher's son whose big moment came when they served chocolate-covered doughnuts after choir practice. And I wasn't going back that route either. If only he weren't such a relic!

I figured that since I was already grounded, this was as good a time as any to tell him about losing my job. He couldn't be any more distressed than he already was, so I told him the whole story. I didn't watch him while I was relating the gory details, and when I finished and looked over at him I nearly passed out. He was laughing so hard that the tears were streaming down his face.

"Don't worry about that, Joseph. I'll speak to Mr. Granger and I'm sure he'll reconsider." He wiped his eyes and blew his nose. "However, perhaps you can see how your own behavior was indirectly responsible for the consequences. If you hadn't left to go to that band practice, none of this would have happened."

I didn't think this was the time to argue that one. Now that Dad's good humor was restored, I made a pass at trying to make him understand my wanting to stay with the band and the frat.

"It's up to you, of course, Joseph, but you know how I feel. My only concern is for your own good. We will say no more about it. Now, hadn't you better get ready for school?" He stood and smiled at me, then walked out of the room, muttering, "Pumpkin pulp! Oh, how I wish I'd seen that!"

I felt really bad about what I was going to do. Dad was a good guy and probably deserved a better son than me — someone on the order of a male Saralee Tidbell. But I had my life to lead and I wasn't going to let him ruin it.

Ten

I drove Woody to school and got him to his first
class. After that he was on his own. I hoped he'd
make it through the day, but I seriously doubted
it. Later in the morning I saw Amy and apologized
again for what happened the night before.

"It's not your fault, Joe, but really, do you have to
hang around with such a gorp?"

"He's not a gorp, Amy," I answered. "He's just not
used to girls."

"Well, he's not going to have a chance to be around
Cookie again, I can tell you that! She's furious — at
me, at you, and mostly at your juvenile friend."

"I can't say I blame her. Anyway, I think Woody's
learned his lesson. Maybe I should have started him off
on someone a little less carnivorous than the Cookie
Monster."

Amy giggled and took my hand. "Let's forget about
Woody, Joe. Can you come over to the house after
practice tonight? I want you to see the dress Mom
brought back from New York for the dance on Friday."

The practice. I'd have to figure out some way to get
out of the house without Dad's finding out. I sure
wasn't going to miss the practice any more than I was

going to quit the frat, but it would have to be done without Dad's knowing. I really didn't want to hurt him any more than I already had. I'd find a way to get to the practice, I promised myself, but going to Amy's afterward was a little more than I could handle right now.

"I'll have to take a rain check on that, Amy," I answered. "The teachers are really piling the work on us, and I'm getting behind."

"Yeah, I guess it is harder in grade 12. Anyway, I'll see you tonight." She reached up and planted a kiss right on my mouth. A couple of passing kids snickered, and my face began to feel as if I'd been out in the sun too long.

* * *

When I arrived at Gord's house that evening, after telling Mom I was going to the library to study, everyone was already there. I rushed in, apologizing for being late, and began to unpack my guitar. When I was settled in my seat I glanced over at Amy and gave her a quick wink. She glared back and turned away. I couldn't figure what was up, but all through practice every time I looked over at her she gave me this icy stare and tossed her head.

It wasn't until two hours later when we were packing up that I found out what the problem was.

"Hey, Amy," I called as she started up the stairs. "Wait up."

She stopped but didn't look at me.

"What gives anyway? You're acting like you heard I've got a social disease."

"You do. You're a snitch. That's the worst social disease going."

"I don't know what you're talking about," I hedged.

"Sure you do. Your dear father was on the phone to my parents first thing to tell them their wicked daughter was corrupting his lily-white son."

Oh, no. Dad really had talked to the Hubanks.

"Amy, I'm sorry. I didn't mean to get you in trouble. Dad woke up last night when we were coming in and saw Woody. He knew we were at your house and just put two and two together." It wasn't exactly true, of course, but it sounded a little better than the actual facts.

The anger faded a little and she made a small grimace. "Well, whatever happened, I've been grounded. They hit me with it when I came home from school this afternoon. No Harvest Dance; no dates at all for a month."

"Me too," I confessed. "Dad even wants me to quit the frat — *and* the band. I'm not going to, of course, but it's likely to get a little dicey when the whole town sees me playing at the Elks dance next Saturday."

"He wants you quit the band? Gee, Joe, what's the matter with your father anyway? He never used to be such a tyrant."

"I don't know. Premature senility maybe." I laughed uneasily. "Anyway, I'm really sorry about the dance. I sure was looking forward to taking you."

"Is there any reason why you still can't?"

"But you said yourself that you were grounded."

"I have no intention of letting that get in the way of going to the dance."

"So what are you going to do?"

"I'll tell the folks that I'm staying the night at a girlfriend's house. It won't be a lie," she hastened to add. "I will be staying with a girlfriend — after the dance."

"Aren't you afraid they'll check up on you?"

"It's not likely. Anyway, it's worth the chance. The Chi Delt Harvest Dance is the biggest social event of the fall. I wouldn't miss it for anything."

I guess I must have looked as stricken as I felt.

"Can't you do the same thing?" Amy asked.

"It wouldn't work for me. Dad said home by ten and he meant *my* home."

"Couldn't you sneak out of the house? Pretend to go to bed early, then when your folks are caught up in TV or something slip out the bedroom window?"

"Amy, my bedroom's on the second floor. I'd probably break both my legs, and that wouldn't help my dancing any!"

She giggled, then shrugged.

"Suit yourself. But if you're not going to take me, tell me now. I can always go to the dance with Paul Gross, you know."

That did it. I'd manage to get away somehow, even if I had to put sleeping pills in their cocoa.

"Of course I'm going to take you. But since I obviously won't be picking you up at your house, you'd better tell me where I'll find you."

"At Cookie Witherspoon's house. Her date will drive us to the dance." She grinned triumphantly, and I had the feeling she had the whole thing planned long before we talked.

"Sounds great. See you later, okay? I've gotta get home and hit the books." I braced myself and bent down to kiss her on the cheek. She turned her head and I got her right on the lips. She didn't back away.

* * *

"Woody called when you were out," Mom announced

when I came in the door a few minutes later. "He said he'd ring you back when he got home from the library." She gave me a funny look. "Did you see him there?"

"No," I answered, feeling the trap snapping at me, "I guess I must have been in another section."

"I see." She went back to her book without further comment, and I went into the kitchen to fix myself a sandwich. A few minutes later the phone rang.

"Hey, Joe, where have you been? Your mom said you were at the library, but I couldn't find you anywhere."

"Later, Woody," I whispered for no particular reason except that I was beginning to feel like a character from a spy novel. "What were you calling about?"

"Mostly to see how it went with your dad — boy, he was really mad — and to apologize for screwing things up so badly."

"Forget it. It wasn't your fault. It was that kookie Cookie. She was enough to make anyone take to drink."

He snickered uncomfortably and cleared his throat. "If there's anything I can to do to help . . ."

"There isn't. Dad's grounded me and suggested very strongly that I'd be better off if I quit the band and the fraternity, but I'm not taking it too seriously."

"Gee, I'm sorry. Boy, when I mess up I do it big, don't I?"

"That you do," I agreed, thinking of the pumpkin fiasco and laughing. "By the way, how do you feel?"

"Like I've been put through a pasta machine. What *did* happen last night anyway, Joe? I really don't remember very much."

"You drank a bottle of sherry, threw up on your date, passed out, and fell down a flight of stairs."

There was silence for a minute. "Oh, is that all?" He chuckled. "I thought it was something serious."

"Woody, you clown!" I laughed. At least *he'd* come through the ordeal relatively unscathed. "Anything else on your mind?"

"Yeah, I heard today from the TV station. They sent me a contract for the program I was telling you about. I do my first show day after tomorrow. Do you think your folks would let you come down to the station with me?"

"I'm sure they wouldn't object about anything that important. That's terrific, Woody. Pretty soon you'll have your own show, and I can tell people I knew you when."

"Yeah, sure. I just hope I don't blow it."

"You won't. You're a pro. See you tomorrow." I hung up and went to my room before Mom had a chance to ask any more uncomfortable questions.

* * *

I told Gord I wouldn't be able to come to practice on Tuesday and went to my first fraternity meeting as a bona fide member. Dad thought I was going to choir practice, of course, so I would be able to stay out past the curfew if necessary.

After we'd gone through all the rituals and most of the business, Cliff announced that Dewie Riceman would not be joining the fraternity after all and that they were looking for a replacement. Nothing was said about why he quit (or was asked to quit) and I didn't think it was my place to probe the issue. It was hard not to show my relief, though. Dewie looked like nothing but trouble for me.

"So do we have any suggestions for a new brother?" Cliff asked.

A couple of names were mentioned and received without much enthusiasm. Then when nobody came up with another name, I put up my hand.

"Yes, Joe? You have a suggestion?"

"Yes. Woody Albert. He's a really nice guy, and I think he would be a great addition to the fraternity."

Aaron Gold nodded. "Yeah, I know Woody. He's a great guy — a little shy, but a real brain."

"We could use a little more Mensa power around here," Cliff said with a grin. "Anyone have any objections to putting his name up for voting?"

"Yeah, I do." A guy whose name I didn't know spoke up. "He's a real jerk. I heard he got so drunk the other night that he threw up all over his date. I don't think we want anyone like that in the fraternity."

There were a few muttered agreements. I tried to explain what had happened with Woody at Amy's house, but I didn't make much of an impression.

"I think we'd better leave the matter pending for the time being," Cliff declared. "There's no rush now. We can't initiate a new member until after the Harvest Dance anyway."

The meeting went on for another half-hour, then we stopped for Cokes and sandwiches. It was a little after ten, so I took off as soon as I could decently get away and was home by ten-thirty.

"Enjoy practice, dear?" Mom called from the living room as I came in the front door.

"It was a gas," I answered and rushed upstairs.

I was getting so good at lying that it was scaring me a little.

Eleven

The next day I went to the TV station with Woody. It's a good thing I did because he was so scared that I practically had to carry him into the studio. However, as soon as he got into his makeup he turned into a different person. As he stood outside camera range waiting for his turn, he could have been Johnny Carson waiting to do his monologue.

As usual, I was blown away by his routine. The studio had a group of about six little kids on the set, and Woody had them in the palm of his hand in about two minutes. One little girl got laughing so hard that she wet her pants. Fortunately the cameraman saw what was happening in time, so her accident wasn't preserved on videotape for posterity.

When he was finished, the producer came over to Woody and shook his hand so hard that I thought it might fall off.

"Amazing! Wonderful! What an asset you're going to be to 'Kid Stuff,'" he enthused.

Woody grinned and looked down at the floor with an "aw, shucks! It weren't nothin'," shrug.

"You must be very proud of your friend." The

producer turned his toothy smile in my direction. "He could go a long way."

"Yeah, I sure am," I answered and realized that it was true. I *was* proud of Woody. He might be a bit of a klutz at times, but he was a very talented guy — and a good friend. I vowed I'd somehow persuade the fraternity to invite him to join.

* * *

I talked to Amy Thursday night after practice about our plans for the next evening. I'd used the old "going to the library to study" routine to get away that night, but I knew it wouldn't work for the dance. Even Dad knows the library doesn't stay open till midnight. I was going to have to come up with another scheme to get out of the house. I didn't have any idea what it would be, but I was determined I'd find a way.

We agreed to meet at Cookie Witherspoon's house at nine o'clock, which meant that I'd have to leave the Women's Shelter about eight-thirty in order to get home, change, and find a way to leave the house without my parents seeing me. I considered asking them if I could stay overnight at Woody's, but I rejected that idea as soon as it was born. As I told Amy, Dad wasn't likely to fall for that, and it could arouse his suspicions. Besides, the last thing I wanted to do was implicate Woody in my slight deception. Okay, so it was a little more than slight. Woody probably would have gone along with my lies, but he would have hated it. I wasn't too happy about it myself, but I just had to get to the dance; my fraternity brothers expected it and so, certainly, did Amy.

Usually we stay at the shelter till about nine, so when

I told Woody I'd be leaving a little early he wanted to know what was up.

"Remember Dad grounded me," I reminded him. "I'm supposed to be home not later than nine o'clock for the next two weeks." Not the gospel truth but close enough.

"Oh, gosh, Joe, I'm so sorry. It's all my fault. Maybe I should have tried to talk to your dad — explain that you weren't to blame."

I want you to know I felt like a real creep. I didn't really want to lie to Woody, but I couldn't tell him I had to get home so I could sneak out to a fraternity dance. One, he'd be disgusted with me for deceiving my parents, and two, he'd feel lousy that I was going to a dance with a girl when he couldn't even manage a casual date.

"It's not your fault, Woody. Dad's getting more unreasonable all the time. I honestly don't know what his problem is, but I think it has to do with his being a minister. No, I don't mean that he's got some stupid idea that he has to protect me from the wages of sin — though on second thought that seems to be part of it. I just think he's beginning to realize how unimportant his job is. People aren't going to church the way they used to, for one thing. He's an anachronism — peddling out-of-date religion to a society that just doesn't buy the fairy tales."

"You're being pretty harsh on him, aren't you, Joe? Your dad is respected in this town by a lot of people."

"Maybe, but not because he's doing anything important. He's a nice guy and people like him. That's all."

Woody didn't offer any more argument, but I don't think he bought my very clever analysis.

* * *

When I got home Mom and Dad were in the living room, as usual, watching a golden oldie on Public. I stopped for a minute to say good-night, and with a lot of loud yawning, I explained that I was beat and was going to bed early.

"Don't you want to watch the film with us, dear?" Mom asked. "It's a Ginger Rogers–Fred Astaire musical."

"Gee, I'd like to — " another yawn " — but I don't think I could keep my eyes open."

"Maybe it's just as well you turn in early, son," Dad agreed. "Mr. Granger will be expecting you at the store by eight-thirty tomorrow morning."

I'd forgotten all about the Saturday job. Dad said he'd fix it with Mr. Granger and I guess he had. The trouble was, I needed to get to practice in the afternoon — Gord was getting a little teed off with me for missing so many the past week — and I sure couldn't ask Woody to fill in for me again. I'd just have to skip practice again and find some excuse to give Gord. I was getting awfully good at that.

As soon as I got to my room I threw my guitar in the corner and began to change into my best cords and the cashmere sweater my aunt sent me last year for Christmas. I brushed my teeth, slapped on some after-shave, and sat down on the bed to figure out what I'd do next. I glanced at my watch: eight-fifty. I'd have to think of something mighty quick. There was no hope of slipping past the living room without Mom and Dad seeing me, and going out the back way was too risky. Dad had the habit of going to the kitchen every so often for something to eat, and with my luck he'd choose the very moment I was sneaking out the back door to have a doughnut attack.

No, my only hope was the window. I went over, opened it, and looked out. The big elm tree was only about four feet from the house. I thought if I was very careful I could reach out to the nearest branch and swing myself over. It was a little risky and if I slipped I could break half the bones in my body, not to mention alert the whole neighborhood to my unusual exit. But I had to take a chance.

I opened the window as wide as it would go and, standing on the edge of the sill, reached out with my right hand for the branch while steadying myself with my left hand on the window frame. When I had the branch firmly I pivoted and threw myself forward, grabbing the branch with my left hand. For a couple of seconds it was touch and go. The branch bent under my weight and I wasn't sure it would hold me. Somehow I got my legs onto the branch below and it took some of the weight. Then I had to reach back to the window and pull it shut. It was late October and quite cold. Someone would certainly feel the draft coming from my room and go in to check. I nearly took a header when I started to pull the window shut, but I caught myself in time and got it closed, then scrambled down to the ground. How I was going to get back in after the dance was something I didn't want to think about right then.

Amy was waiting for me in the back of Cookie's boyfriend's car when I arrived, panting, a little after nine. Cookie greeted me with her "gee whiz" giggle and introduced me to her date. It was the guy in my fraternity who had told everyone about Woody getting sick. At least now I knew where he got his information.

* * *

The dance was being held in a private golf club. One of the guys in the fraternity had a father who was a member, so he was able to get us a deal. I hadn't been involved in the preparations for the dance since I was new, so I didn't know what to expect. It was sheer class. Someone had taken a lot of trouble with the decorations; there were haystacks in the corners, pumpkins and sheaves of wheat and all sorts of other harvesty stuff scattered around the room, and balloons everywhere. A five-piece band was playing soft rock in the corner and the two tables along the front were loaded with food and drinks.

Amy and I danced every dance except for the ones we sat out in the deserted room we found down the corridor. We took a couple of plates of food and when we'd demolished them we did a little stint of heavy breathing. It was great.

The dance officially ended at midnight when the caretaker at the club shooed us all out. Jimbo (Cookie's date) drove Amy and Cookie home. Amy and I said good-night for half an hour or so on Cookie's front porch while Cookie and Jimbo made out in the car.

When the girls had gone in, Jimbo motioned for me to get back in the car. I told him I could walk home easily, but he just laughed and said, "You've got to be kidding. Hop in."

Wanting to get on his good side in order to change his mind about Woody, I hopped in. I gave him my address but he just laughed again and allowed as how I must still be kidding as he roared off in the opposite direction.

We went through town and out into the country where

an old roadside inn dating back to the fifties had just reopened. I'd heard a little about it, but it wasn't the kind of place my former acquaintances — Saralee Tidbell and her ilk — frequented. When we went in we found most of our fraternity brothers gathered around a big table in the middle of the room watching the floor show.

As we slipped into chairs in the darkened room, Sam Quan, who was sitting next to me, whispered, "Isn't she something? Her name is Bunny Hug — can you believe it?"

I couldn't; nor could I believe what she was doing with her unclothed body. I'm not a drinker but at that moment I needed something to calm me down. I ordered a double rye from the topless waitress leaning over me and looked around the room. All I needed now was for someone who knew my dad to see me there. However, the clientele, I decided, weren't the type who likely attended church regularly. I finished my rye just about the time Bunny Hug finished her acrobatics and the lights came up.

I ordered another double rye and downed it in two gulps.

"You should have been here earlier," Aaron Gold drooled. "There were these two girls, Cara Milk and Jackie Cracker . . ." I got up and went to the washroom.

The rye hit me pretty hard and I stayed in the washroom for about fifteen minutes, trying to stop the wall from falling in on me. When I came back most of the guys were dancing with girls that they'd apparently picked up at the bar. I caught Jimbo's eye and when he came over to see what I wanted I asked him how much longer he was planning to stay.

"Hey, Joe, the night's young," he answered. "Find yourself a piece of flesh and join the crowd." He leered at me and danced off with someone in pink garters and sequined underwear.

I checked out the rest of my brothers; they were all either drunk or otherwise engaged. It didn't look as though any of them were planning to leave for a very long time.

I had a choice: I could wait around for a ride home or I could call a cab. I decided that even though it would cost the better part of a day's wages at Granger's I'd go for the cab.

It was two-fifteen when I started to shimmy up the old elm tree and two-thirty when I finally managed to get the window open and crawl through.

As I lay in bed too wound up to sleep, I thought about the evening. The dance had been terrific, but the scene at the roadhouse had kind of spoiled things. I knew the guys in the frat were just having fun — no harm done — but it wasn't my idea of a good time.

I wanted to belong to the fraternity and I liked most of the guys who were my brothers, but I just wasn't comfortable doing some of the things they did. That's what comes of being a preacher's kid, I thought. Always odd man out. Once a Holy Joe always a Holy Joe. Why couldn't I have been born the son of a barber? But damn it all, I didn't have to be different. Did I?

Twelve

I didn't get to sleep for a couple of hours as I lay
there tossing and turning. When Mom knocked on
the door to tell me it was time to get up, I felt as
if I'd just gone to sleep. I wanted more than anything
to say I wasn't feeling well, then turn over and die for
the next ten hours, but this was not the day to pull a
"too sick to work" number. So I crawled out of bed,
turned the shower on cold, and tried to get my body
back to something like normal.

When I got down to breakfast, the rest of the family
was already eating. I slumped into my chair, and Mom
slid a plate of fried eggs in front of me. I looked down;
they looked back. Suddenly, the contents of my stomach lurched up into my throat screaming, "Let us out!"
I swallowed, took a bite of toast, and tried to look as
though I felt just dandy.

I finished the toast and half a cup of tea and began
feeling that I might live. It was all going to work out
after all. I'd managed to get out of the house and back
in without anyone being the wiser. I had my job back.
Amy had agreed to go steady last night. I was on top
of the world.

Then Marty spoke.

"I'll put your guitar back in your room right after breakfast, Joe. Thanks a lot for lending it to me last night."

My head shot up and I stared at her. She had this smug expression on her face and was smiling knowingly at me.

"My guitar?"

"Yes. Don't you remember I came to your room last night after you'd gone to bed and borrowed it. You were so nice to let me use it."

"Yeah, sure," I mumbled as I tried to sort out the meaning of this unwelcome announcement.

So Marty had come into my room and found me gone. Why hadn't she said anything? Marty isn't a snitch generally, but it wasn't like her not to blurt out, Where were you last night when I was looking for you? or something equally devastating.

"Oh, was that you, Marty?" Mom asked. "I heard the guitar last night and thought it was Joe. You're getting to be quite good."

The great feeling I had disappeared as quickly as it had come. Marty obviously wanted something, and the sooner I found out what it was the better.

"If I may be excused, I think I'd better get my stuff and head for the store," I said, and quickly left the room. Marty wasn't far behind.

"So why didn't you tell the folks I wasn't in my room last night?" I asked, closing my bedroom door and turning to face her.

"I figured you didn't want them to know, of course. I was just protecting you, big brother."

"Okay, so why bring it up at all?"

"Well, I just wanted you to know I was doing you a

big favor, then maybe you wouldn't mind doing me one in return."

"Mary Martha Larriby, you're blackmailing me!"

"Not a nice word. Let's just say we're exchanging favors."

"So what's the favor?"

Marty dropped onto my bed and crossed her legs under her, yoga-style.

"Well," she began, getting comfortable, "there's this party tonight at Rita Gamble's house, and I want to go, but Dad says I'm too young to be, quote, tearing around with that older crowd, unquote."

"Maybe he's right, Marty. Rita *is* a couple of years older and," I added, "more experienced."

"Not you too, Joe! I thought you'd finally grown out of your goody-goody attitude, but I guess I was wrong. Good old Holy Joe!"

I looked down at her and saw the tears forming in her eyes. I felt like an ogre. All she wanted to do was go to a harmless little house party put on by a fifteen-year-old and I was coming on as if she wanted to join a coven.

"So what do you want me to do?" I sighed. "Talk to Dad?"

"You know that wouldn't do any good. No, I want you to cover for me while I sneak in and out of the house." The tears had dried up and she was smiling happily. "It's no big deal; all you have to do is get the parents out of the way while I slip out of the house, then be around to let me in when I come home. I'll pretend to go to bed early — just like you did — and they'll never know the difference. As a matter of fact, you could stop by my room sometime during the evening and pretend to be talking to me." She looked anxiously up at me, still smiling. "Will you do it?"

"And if I don't?"

The smile disappeared. She looked down at her knees and began picking at a scab. "Don't worry; I won't rat on you even if you don't help me."

That, of course, was all I needed to make up my mind. God knows I was fed up enough with Dad's overly strict rules. How could I break them, then expect my sister to stick to them? Besides, I told myself again, it was just an innocent little house party.

"What time do you want to go and when will you be home?" I asked.

She jumped up from the bed and threw her arms around me. "Does that mean you'll help me?"

"Yeah, sure. But you mustn't be too late. It'll look darn funny if I'm sitting around the living room till all hours waiting to let you in."

"I won't be late, I promise. The party starts about eight. I should be home by eleven."

"Okay, that shouldn't be a problem." I looked at my watch and grabbed my jacket. "I've gotta get going. The last thing I need today is to be late for work. See you tonight." I gave her a peck on the cheek and raced out of the room.

* * *

Mr. Granger was real nice about taking me back. I guess after he cooled off he realized the Great Pumpkin Pile-up wasn't exactly my fault.

"But, Joe," he said, as he handed me the keys to the van, "please don't ever get that . . . that *person* to fill in for you again. If you can't make it, just let me know a little ahead of time and I'll get someone more reliable. Like old Stan from the church," he muttered.

Gord, however, wasn't so nice when I told him I wouldn't be able to make practice again that afternoon.

"For pete's sake, Joe, the dance is just a week off. We need all the practice together we can get." He sounded exasperated and I didn't blame him. But there was no way I could leave the job — not after last week's fiasco.

"I promise to be at every rehearsal from tomorrow on, Gord. I'll even miss my fraternity meeting on Tuesday and the Doodles on Friday."

"Well, okay, but I'm going to hold you to it. This gig means too much to all of us for one person to screw it up."

I was getting in so deep that I wondered if I'd ever get out. Not only was I grounded but I had too many conflicting demands going on at the same time. Things, I decided, were a lot calmer when I was still the skinny little preacher's kid.

Then there was Amy. Although she was grounded too, she thought we should try to find a way to get together that night. I had to tell her no way — not only was I still recuperating from sneaking out the night before, but I had to be available to help Marty. She took it pretty well, but I had the feeling she thought I was being a bit of a wimp.

* * *

Getting Marty out of the house turned out to be a piece of cake. When dinner was over, we all congregated in the living room to watch TV. Fortunately one of Dad's favorite nature programs came on at seven, so it was perfectly natural for Marty to announce that she wasn't interested and that she thought she'd go to bed and read. At seven-thirty, when the program was over, I suggested we go into Dad's den and play Scrabble. Dad jumped at the chance, but Mom said she thought she'd just stay in the living room and read.

"Oh, Mom!" I exclaimed, trying not to sound desperate. "You've gotta come too. You're the only one who can catch Dad cheating!"

Mom laughed and, to my total relief, got up and went into the den. I closed the door and prayed Marty wouldn't bang into anything getting out of the house.

We played three games of Scrabble, all of which Dad won in spite of Mom's watchful eye and the unabridged Webster's dictionary.

"Well, well," Dad said, beaming as he totaled up the score of the last game, "I guess we know who's the winner and still champion, don't we?"

Mom just smiled and packed up the board. "Let's all have a cup of cocoa," she suggested, "then get to bed. Sunday is always so busy."

I very quickly agreed and even made the cocoa myself. By ten o'clock they were up in their room. I had one scary moment when Mom said she thought she'd check on Marty; she didn't want her reading till all hours.

"Never mind!" I cried. Calming down a little, I added, "I'll go." I raced upstairs and made a big pretense of opening Marty's door and calling to her, then quickly closing the door as Mom came to the top of the stairs.

"She's asleep," I whispered.

Mom nodded and went on down to her bedroom

without stopping. A moment later my heart began beating again.

I went back downstairs and turned on the TV. This was pretty normal behavior for me on a Saturday night, so Mom and Dad had no reason to be suspicious of anything. Everything had gone perfectly. I lay down on the couch and tuned in a "Simon and Simon" rerun while I waited for Marty.

* * *

I guess the four hours of sleep I'd had the night before began to tell on me because I zonked out halfway through the program and when I woke up the news was just winding up. I looked at my watch: eleven fifty-five. I started to curse Marty for being late, then I panicked, thinking she'd probably come home and couldn't make me hear her.

I ran to the front door, expecting to see her shivering and furious on the front step. No one was there. Now I really did panic. My first impulse was to call out for her, but that would only have wakened Mom and Dad. Besides, I reasoned, why would she be within shouting distance? She must have come home and when I didn't let her in she went back to Rita's house.

I closed the door and ran to get the phone book. I was so nervous that I could hardly see the numbers. Finally, I found what I was looking for: J. Y. Gamble 555-4598. I dialed the number and prayed Rita would answer. I didn't feel up to explaining to her father or mother why I was trying to find my sister.

"Rita?"

"Yes, who's this?"

"Joe Larriby. Is Marty there?"

"No, Joe, she left a couple of hours ago. Isn't she home yet?"

"No, she's not. I thought she might have had trouble getting in the house and gone back to your place."

There was a pause on the other end of the line. Then Rita spoke, her voice hesitant.

"Marty left with a boy she met at the party, Joe. I didn't know him; he came with another guy I'd invited. He was going to drive her home, or so he said. I was a little worried 'cause I think he'd been drinking."

Oh, my God! What if Marty had got herself into something she couldn't handle. After all, she was only thirteen. "Rita, do you know where this guy lives?"

"I've no idea. But maybe Jay knows; he's the one who brought him. He left a few minutes ago, but I can phone him. I'll call you right back if I find out anything."

She hung up and I sat with the receiver in my hand for a couple of minutes before I realized what I was doing. I hung it up and waited.

Five interminable minutes later the phone rang. I grabbed it and shouted, "Rita?"

"Jay wasn't home, Joe. I guess he and a bunch of the guys went somewhere after the party. Look, is there anything I can do?"

"Not really, Rita. Just keep trying to get hold of Jay, eh?"

"Sure," she answered, sounding very concerned. "Maybe you'd better speak to your folks, Joe. Marty told me they didn't know she was coming to the party, but don't you think they should know she's not home?"

That's all I needed — for the folks to know Marty had sneaked out of the house and I'd helped her.

"I'll give it another fifteen minutes, Rita. If I don't hear from you by then I'll wake them."

But I didn't have to wait fifteen minutes. Less than five minutes later the phone rang.

"Rita?" I hollered. "Did you get hold of Jay?"

"This is Sergeant Yarrow, City Police," the voice on the phone answered. "Is this the home of Dr. Rupert Larriby?"

I swallowed and managed a weak yes.

"May I speak to Dr. Larriby, please."

"He's asleep. May I take a message? I'm his son."

"Very well. Please tell him that his daughter has been in an auto accident. She's in the general hospital. Have him come down immediately."

Thirteen

Dad didn't ask any questions at all when I went upstairs and woke him with the terrible news. He just got out of bed, pulled his pants and shirt over his pajamas, and said, "What hospital did the officer say she was in?"

Meanwhile, Mom had run out of their bedroom crying, "There must be some mistake. Marty's in her room asleep."

When she returned a few minutes later, her face was white and she was shaking all over. "I don't understand," she said. "I don't understand."

Dad grabbed his keys from the dresser and said, "Marcella, you wait here. I'll call you from the hospital. Joseph, you come with me."

Dad didn't speak at all as we roared down the road to the hospital. He must have wondered why I was still dressed but he didn't ask. I knew I was going to have a lot of explaining to do, but at that moment all I could think about was Marty.

The woman at the reception desk checked her computer and informed us that Marty was on the third floor. We tore up the stairs, not waiting for the elevator, and as we raced down the hall we nearly collided with Dr. Barker.

"John," Dad said, "Marty's been in an accident. Have you seen her?"

"Yes, Rupert." He paused, then indicated a bench along the wall. "Perhaps we'd better sit down."

Dad kind of staggered over to the bench and collapsed. "Tell me the truth, John. How bad is it?"

"We're not sure. She's still unconscious. No bones are broken and we don't think there are any internal injuries. But she has a bad head injury. We won't know anything until she regains consciousness."

While the doctor was explaining Marty's condition, a police officer walked over to where we were sitting.

"Dr. Larriby? I'm Sergeant Yarrow."

Dad stood up and nodded. "Yes, Sergeant. Could you tell me what happened?"

"Apparently the car your daughter was in went out of control and hit a telephone pole. Your daughter was sitting in the front passenger seat and was thrown against the windshield. Her companion had been drinking, apparently. He was wearing a seat belt and escaped with a few minor cuts and bruises. Your daughter wasn't wearing hers."

"I see." Dad turned back to Dr. Barker. "May I see her?"

"You can go in for a moment, Rupert, but I must warn you. She's hooked up to a lot of instruments and her head is swathed in bandages."

Dad just nodded and Dr. Barker led him to a room at the other end of the hall. I stayed with the police officer. Neither of us spoke.

When Dad returned a few minutes later, he looked as if he'd aged about twenty years. Dr. Barker took his arm and said, "Sit down, Rupert. I'll get you a cup of coffee."

Dad slumped back down on the bench, then a moment later jumped to his feet.

"I must call Marcella. She'll be out of her mind with worry."

When he returned from the phone he handed me the car keys and said, "Go and get your mother, Joseph."

I took the keys and left the hospital.

* * *

"Joe, what in heaven's name is going on?" Mom and I were driving back to the hospital, and Mom, unlike Dad, was full of questions. "Marty went up to her room right after dinner, remember? She said she was going to bed to read. She must have slipped out of the house when we were in the den. But where did she go?"

Her questions weren't exactly directed at me — mostly she was talking to herself. I suppose I could have pretended I knew nothing about Marty's escapade — what was one more lie? — but I knew I had to tell her the truth.

"She went to a house party at Rita Gamble's."

"A house party? Yes, I remember. She asked her father if she could go and he forbade it. But she went anyway?"

"Yes. You were right; she slipped out of the house when we were playing Scrabble."

"I see." Pause. "No, I don't see. How do you know all this, Joe?"

"I helped her." I was gripping the steering wheel so tight that my hands were cramping. I stared straight ahead and waited for her to say something. But she didn't speak.

"Mom!" I cried, when the silence got too heavy to bear. "Don't you understand? I helped Marty disobey you and now she's in the hospital with God knows what kind of injury. And it's my fault."

She continued to stare silently ahead, giving no indication that she'd heard a word I'd said.

I swung the car into the hospital parking lot and slammed on the breaks. She was out the door and running toward the emergency entrance before the motor died.

* * *

The three of us were sitting in the hospital coffee shop playing at eating breakfast. It was eight o'clock and we were all totally destroyed from fear, lack of sleep, worry. Dad had phoned Mr. Granger to give him the news and arrange for him to find someone to take the church service that morning. Up till then he hadn't questioned me, but after the waitress took our uneaten food away and refilled our coffee cups, he spoke.

"What do you know about this, Joseph? Did Marty tell you she was going out last night?"

I took a deep breath and nodded. "Yes, I knew. I helped her slip out without you seeing her by getting you into the den for that Scrabble game."

Dad frowned, his eyes full of confusion. "But why? Joseph, it isn't like you to practice such deception."

"I did it because Marty knew I'd sneaked out of the house the night before when you thought I'd gone to bed early. I went to a fraternity party with Amy Hubank, who also had to sneak out because she had been grounded after you told her folks about Woody."

Dad was still looking as if he didn't or couldn't believe a word I was saying.

"Maybe you'd better tell us everything, Joe," Mom suggested, taking my hand and smiling gently.

So I told them. Everything from the first time I missed choir practice to go to Gord's to visiting the roadhouse and getting high on rye.

"So that's about it," I finished. Strangely enough, I felt better than I had for weeks. It was as though a heavy pack had been lifted from my back and I could stand straight again.

"So Marty made you help her in return for her silence," Dad said. "That's certainly as bad as anything you did, Joseph."

"No, Dad, it wasn't like that at all," I hastened to explain. "Marty told me she found out I wasn't home when she came to borrow my guitar, then she asked me to help her get to the party. But when I asked her if she was going to squeal on me if I didn't help her, she admitted that she wouldn't. No, Dad, I helped her because I thought you were being too strict." I turned to Mom. "So you see, I was right; it *is* my fault that Marty's up in that bed unconscious and . . . and . . ." I couldn't finish. The tears had started and I couldn't stop them.

Mom put her arm around me and made soothing sounds. Dad slumped down in his chair and muttered, "Where did I go so wrong?" He sounded like a character out of a bad movie, but he also sounded as though he meant it.

At that moment I wished with all my heart that I could go back to the beginning of the school year and start all over again. Boy! Would I do things different!

Or would I?

* * *

Dr. Barker insisted we all go home and get some rest. It was after two and Marty was still unconscious. Mom tried to argue but he insisted.

"There's nothing you can do here, Marcella. I'll call you the minute she wakes up, I promise. There's no point in your wearing yourself out; it won't help Marty one bit." He dug in his jacket pocket and handed Dad a little bottle of pills. "Here, give one of these to Marcella and take one yourself."

So we were back at the house. Mom finally broke down about three o'clock and took one of the pills and was upstairs sleeping. Dad was in the den making phone calls to our out-of-town relatives.

When I heard him hang up, I got on the hall phone and called Rita Gamble.

"Joe, I've been worried," she said when she heard my voice. "Did Marty get home okay last night?"

"Marty's in hospital, Rita," I answered as calmly as I could. "The guy that she went off with piled his car into a telephone post. You mentioned that he'd been drinking. Right?"

"Oh, Joe, how horrible! Yes, he'd been drinking all right. Oh, God! I should never have let her go off with him, but you know Marty. She's got a mind of her own."

"Rita, I want to know the guy's name."

"What are you going to do, Joe?" She sounded scared.

"Never mind. Just tell me his name. If you don't I'll get it from the police."

"Okay. I found out from Jay last night. I tried to call you back but there was no answer. It was a kid called Dewie Riceman. I don't know him very well. He wasn't invited to the party; as I told you, Jay brought him."

"Thanks, Rita." I hung up before she could ask me any more questions.

I was putting on my jacket and heading for the door when Dad came into the hall.

"Joseph, where are you going?"

"Out. I have some unfinished business to attend to."

He walked over to me and took my arm. "No, Joseph, punishing the boy who drove the car isn't going to accomplish anything. I'm sure the police will deal with him appropriately. Your going after him will merely compound matters."

"Dad, please don't give me that 'turn the other cheek' crap. That little creep hurt my sister and I'm going to see he hurts real bad in return."

"I know how you feel, Joseph, and it's perfectly natural. But believe me that 'turn the other cheek crap' is the most practical and sensible thing you can do. Please trust me on this one."

I shook his arm away. He didn't understand. Maybe he could forgive and forget — after all, that's what he'd been preaching all his life — but I couldn't. As I buttoned up my jacket I snuck a quick look at him. His face was all blotchy and his eyes had a half-pleading, half-anxious look. It was unbelievable. His daughter was in intensive care at the hospital, no one knowing whether she would live or die, and here he was all concerned about the creep that put her there.

I turned quickly away and threw open the front door.

Fourteen

Dad's car was still parked at the curb where he had left it when we came home a few hours before. Without much hope I checked to see if by any chance he'd left the keys in the ignition. He's usually very careful about removing them and locking up the car, but I guess the strain he was under made him forget. Anyway, there were the keys just where he'd left them. I opened the door, jumped into the driver's seat, and started the engine. As I was racing down the street I glanced in the rearview mirror and saw Dad standing on the porch gesturing at me to come back. I kept right on driving.

When I got to the corner I realized I didn't have the foggiest idea where Dewie Riceman lived. I supposed I could stop at the nearest phone booth and look up the address, but I didn't know his father's name. It could be a dead end.

But I did know where Rita lived. I whipped the car around the corner and headed down the next street. In less than five minutes I was ringing her doorbell.

"Joe!" Rita cried when she saw me standing on her doorstep. "I've been so worried. I called the hospital after you told me what had happened to Marty, but they wouldn't tell me anything. Is she going to be all right?"

"No one knows yet, Rita," I answered impatiently. "Look, I need to get Dewie Riceman's address. Do you have it?"

At that moment a tall guy with a scowl on his face appeared behind Rita.

"What's going on?" he demanded, resting his hand possessively on Rita's shoulder.

Rita half turned and gave him a weak smile. "This is Joe Larriby, Jay. Marty's brother."

"Oh, geez, I'm sorry." The scowl turned to pity. "If there's anything I can do . . ."

"There is," I answered abruptly. "Tell me where Dewie Riceman lives. I take it he's a friend of yours."

The tall guy looked as scared as Rita. "Yeah, he is, sort of." He hesitated, obviously wondering how much he could get away with not telling me.

"Look," I jumped in. "I'll find out one way or another. I just want to talk to the guy — find out what happened."

Jay didn't look too convinced, but I guess he realized I wasn't kidding around.

"Okay," he answered a moment later. "He lives over on Briar Crescent — 143. It's a big brick two-story about the middle of the block." He licked his lips nervously. "I'd be glad to show you," he offered hopefully.

Without bothering to answer, I turned and ran back to the car.

I found the house without much trouble. As a matter of fact, Dewie was coming down the steps just as I was cruising by. I swerved into the curb, stopped the car, and jumped out.

"Hey, Riceman!" I shouted as I rounded the front of the car and ran toward him. "I want to talk to you."

When he saw me he turned abruptly and started for the house, but I caught up with him before he could make it to the front door. I grabbed him by the arm and practically dragged him back to the car.

"Get in," I ordered, opening the passenger door and giving him a shove.

"I can't leave the house," he protested as he fell into the seat. "My dad's lawyer is on his way over. I have to be around when he gets here."

"This'll only take a few minutes." I slammed the door, ran around to the other side, and slid under the wheel. Two minutes later I was parking the car beside a picnic table in the deserted park a few blocks away.

"Okay, get out," I ordered, leaning across and opening his door. I jumped out and walked over to the table. Dewie followed fearfully. "Sit down."

Dewie sat. I stood over him, looking down. Now that I had him there, I wasn't sure what I was going to do. I guess he saw the hesitation on my face. The fear left his eyes and he gave me a sneering smile.

"So what are you going to do, jellyfish?" He smirked. "Try to scare a confession out of me? The cops know what happened. Your dumb sister tried to take the wheel from me and ran us into a tree. They've got nothing on me."

"I don't believe you," I half whispered. "You were drunk. Rita said so."

"Oh, I may have had a beer or two. I wasn't drunk. But that hot little piece, Marty, sure was."

I could feel myself getting angrier and angrier. I knew I had to keep my cool, but it was getting more and more difficult.

"Marty doesn't drink. You were smashed and you rammed the car into a telephone pole. Because of you, Marty's in intensive care at the hopital. They don't know if she'll make it or not."

"Look, it's not my fault! Now quit trying to be Perry Mason and drive me back home. My dad's lawyer will get me off without even a reprimand."

Judging by the size of his house, I figured Dewie's father was probably rolling in it. He'd get a fancy lawyer and Dewie *would* get off scot-free. My cool was beginning to disappear very quickly.

"Maybe," I said. "But you're going to pay for what you did to my sister, even if I have to do it myself."

"Oh, come on, jellyfish. You haven't got the guts to step on a slug." He sat back against the table and grinned knowingly. "Holy Joe, the preacher's son. Have you any idea what a laughingstock you are around the school? I suppose you think you're hot stuff since you got invited to join the Chi Delts. Well, I have a news flash for you: they only asked you because they needed to add a few 'brains.' And Amy Hubank is telling everyone what a jerk you are and how she only dates you for laughs." I stared dumbfounded at him, unable to speak. He settled more comfortably against the table and, looking very pleased with himself, continued.

"You and that creep Woody Albert are the joke of the school. Just like your old man is the joke of the town."

The last of my cool disappeared. I grabbed Dewie by the shirtfront and pulled him to his feet.

"You're a damned liar!" I shouted. "The Chi Delts kicked you out of the frat!"

Dewie looked a little less sure of himself as I began to twist his shirt collar.

"Not true!" he gagged. "My folks made me quit. The guys begged me to stay but my dad said my grades weren't good enough."

"Another damned lie!" I twisted the collar tighter. Dewie's face began to turn red.

"Hey, you stupid jerk, you're hurting me!" he gurgled. "Just because your round-heeled sister got herself in trouble, you don't need to choke me to death."

That did it. I gave his collar another twist, then grabbed his head with my other hand and smashed his face down on the table. Blood gushed from his nose. I lifted his head and was just about to smack it down again when I heard a scream. I turned around and saw Amy's terrified face looking up at me. Woody was standing a couple of feet behind her. I held Dewie for a second or two longer, then let go and sank to the ground.

Dewie got up slowly and wiped his face with his sleeve. Seeing the blood, he began to scream. "Look what you did, you stupid oaf! You broke my nose! Boy, wait'll my dad's lawyer hears about this!"

"You nose isn't broken, Dewie," Woody muttered, coming over to stand beside me. "Now get the hell out of here before I take you on myself."

Under ordinary circumstances this would have broken me up. Woody is about six inches shorter and thirty pounds lighter than Dewie. But these weren't ordinary circumstances. Dewie looked as frightened of Woody as he did of me. With another swipe at his nose, which had now stopped bleeding, and another "You just wait. You'll get yours," he ran across the park to the highway.

Amy came up to me and took my hand. "Come on, Joe, let's get out of here and find someplace we can talk."

I nodded and Woody and I followed her back to the car. Their bikes were lying on the ground where they had obviously thrown them when they saw me trying to murder Dewie Riceman. Woody reached down and folded them up, then wordlessly gestured for the keys to the trunk. I tossed them to him, still half dazed. After he'd stashed the bikes away he started to hand the keys back to me. I shook my head and slipped into the passenger seat. "You'd better drive," I muttered. "I don't think I'm up to it."

Fifteen

Woody turned onto the highway and started to head back to my house.

"Not yet, Woody," I said when I saw where we were going. "Let's stop for a Coke. I don't want to go home just yet."

Without a word he made an illegal U-turn in the middle of the highway and drove quickly to the shopping mall a few blocks away.

When we were seated in a back booth at the A & W with colas and a plate of fries in front of us, Woody finally spoke.

"Okay, what's going on? Why were you trying to singlehandedly demolish Dewie Riceman's face?"

I took a long swig of my drink and looked away. "How did you know where to find me?" I asked without answering his question.

"I went over to your house to see if you wanted to go to the science museum. Your dad told me what had happened to Marty and that you left the house half crazy. He was afraid you were going to find the guy who caused the accident and, as he put it, wreak your own form of vengeance. I guess he was right."

"I guess so. Go on."

"He said you had talked to someone called Rita. I figured I'd better go after you, but I didn't know any Rita. I was standing outside your house trying to figure out what to do when Amy rode up."

Amy took over at that point.

"Rita had called me and told me about Marty. I came over as soon as I heard. We jumped on our bikes and rode to her house to find you. You'd just left, she said, and had gone to Dewie Riceman's house. When we got there we saw your car driving off."

"We couldn't keep up with you, of course," Woody continued, "but you seemed to be heading for the park, so we took our chances and followed you there. You know the rest." He bit into a fry and looked at me. "Okay, now your turn."

"It all started when I snuck out of the house to go to the dance," I began. Then for the next ten minutes I poured out the whole story. The only thing I didn't tell them was the stuff Dewie said about Woody — the guy didn't need to hear that kind of junk. "I don't think I really meant to hurt Dewie," I finished, "but when he started saying those things about Marty I went crazy. She's lying in a hospital bed unconscious; she may die, and he's going to go scot-free."

Woody kept picking at the fries and watching me. "And you feel guilty as hell for helping her get to the party. Right?"

"Right," I murmured, looking down to avoid his eyes.

"Look, Joe, I know you won't believe me right now, but you aren't to blame for what happened. Marty would have found a way to get to that party whether you helped her or not. You know that. And as for Marty being drunk and all the rest of that crap, you can't believe anything a creep like Dewie Riceman says."

I looked back up at Woody. He was peering anxiously at me through his huge glasses. His enormous nose was red and his chin was quivering. The guy was really concerned about me. I began to feel a little better. I was letting the stuff Dewie said get to me, and as Woody pointed out, Dewie's word wasn't exactly sacred.

I gave him a tentative smile and drained my glass.

"Thanks, pal," I said. "And not just for the pep talk. Thanks for keeping me from doing something stupid at the park."

Woody looked uncomfortable and shrugged. "Nothing," he muttered and finished off the last of the fries.

I had been so absorbed in Woody that I hadn't noticed how quiet Amy had become. When I turned to look at her I was shocked to see tears streaming down her face.

"Woody's right, Joe. It isn't your fault. It's mine. And I don't think I'll ever be able to forgive myself, let alone expect you to forgive me."

"Don't be dumb, Amy," I answered. "How could it possibly be your fault?"

"Don't you see?" She took a deep breath and swallowed a sob. "If I hadn't insisted you sneak out so we could go to that stupid dance, none of this would ever have happened. Marty wouldn't have had anything to hold over you to make you help her sneak out."

"No, Amy, you're wrong." Woody shook his head. "It's like I just told Joe: Marty would have found a way to get to that dance with or without Joe's help. Nobody's to blame, and it's time you both got that through your thick heads."

I don't think I'd ever heard Woody lay down the law to anyone before. I'm darn sure Amy hadn't. We looked at each other, then at Woody. "Right," we answered in unison.

Woody blushed right down to his scrawny ankles.

I guess everything would have turned out differently if at that moment Cliff Fortana hadn't walked in. He spotted us just as we were getting ready to leave and came over to our table.

"Joe, I just heard the news about Marty. God, I'm so sorry." He slipped into the booth beside Woody. "Is there anything I can do?" he asked

"No, but thanks anyway," I answered, settling back in my seat. It looked as if I was going to have to go through the whole story again. I was right.

"What happened?" Cliff asked after he'd caught the waitress's eye and given his order.

I gave him a condensed version of the story without mentioning my confrontation with Dewie Riceman.

"Was Dewie hurt?" Cliff asked when I had finished.

"No way!" I answered angrily. "He got out of it with a few minor cuts and bruises. What a creep!"

Cliff nodded. "Yeah, you're right. I never thought he was going to be good for the frat, although some of the guys figured he could be a big asset, what with his dad's bucks. Frankly, I was glad when he told us he'd have to resign. Something about his marks being pretty bad and his folks lowering the boom on his social life."

I could feel my mouth start to drop open as I took in his words.

"You mean Dewie quit the frat voluntarily?"

"Of course." Cliff looked surprised at the question.

It took my brain a moment or two to process this information, then when it finally registered I stood up and walked, or more accurately stumbled, down the aisle. Woody ran to catch up to me as I reached the door. I pushed him aside, opened it, and hurried to my car.

"Joe, what's got into you?" I heard him call as I started the motor and roared off.

I had no idea where I was going, but I guess my subconscious took over. I drove blindly down the highway, Cliff's words rushing through my head. Dewie had to quit the frat. Before realizing where I was heading, I found myself up at the top of Scotchman's Hill, the front bumper of the car against the guardrail. It was the exact spot where Amy and I had parked the night I took her to the movies. It seemed about ten years had passed since that night, but I realized it was only a little over a week ago. Everything had seemed so right, then. Now I realized I'd been living in a stupid romantic haze.

Everything Dewie had said to me at the park came back to me in a rush. I was so sure he was lying just to put me down. But I was wrong. He had been telling the truth about leaving the frat voluntarily, therefore didn't it follow that he was telling the truth about everything else? Like Amy going out with me for laughs? Dad being the town joke? The Chi Delts pledging me because of my grades? I remembered how Cliff had mentioned that the frat could use more Mensa power when I'd put Woody up for membership. So that was true too.

Dewie was right! I'd been fooling myself all this time, thinking I'd suddenly changed from being nothing to Big Man on Campus. I'd always be Holy Joe, the jellyfish.

Then I thought about what I'd nearly done to Dewie. If Woody and Amy hadn't come around when he did, I might have really hurt him. Even — I turned cold at the thought — killed him. What kind of a monster was I anyway? It wasn't enough that I was directly responsible for my sister being in a life-or-death situation. No, I had to try to waste someone else just to get even. Mr. Riceman's lawyer was probably filing charges against me that very minute. That's all Mom and Dad needed right then.

My thoughts strayed again to the night up there with Amy and the story she'd told me about the two people who had jumped over the cliff. I remembered how at the time I'd thought it was such a stupid thing to do. Now it started to have a certain appeal.

It would take so little to solve everything. Release the brake, a little pressure on the gas pedal, and it would be all over with. Everyone would think it was an accident.

"He was very upset when he left," I could hear Woody explaining. "He must have misjudged the distance and gone over the edge." The explanation would be accepted without question. After all, preachers' kids don't commit suicide. It's practically a law.

I turned on the motor and let out the hand brake. I put the car in low and started to press down on the accelerator. The car eased forward and hit the guardrail. I gave it a little more gas and the rail moved slightly. All I needed to do was slam down on the accelerator and I'd be over the edge.

But I didn't. I took my foot off the gas pedal and sat staring into space. It was as though I were somewhere else looking at myself sitting there. Why didn't I just go ahead and send the car and myself over the edge? It wasn't because I was afraid — I knew that without a doubt. In fact, the idea became more appealing the more I thought about it. The end to all my troubles.

Sure, and the beginning of everyone else's.

What the hell was I doing? Proving that everything Dewie said about me was true? Maybe I *was* still a wimp, but that was no excuse to take the coward's way out. Dad and Mom needed me as they'd never needed me before. And so did Marty. No way could I let what Dewie or Amy or anyone else in the damn town thought about me make me hurt my family any more than I had. I'd just have to accept that in the eyes of the real winners like Amy and Cliff I was a loser, but so what? Woody thought I was okay, and right now his opinion meant more to me than anyone else's except my family's.

Then there was the stuff Dewie said about Marty — that she had been drinking and was coming on to him. No way was that true. I knew my sister, and Marty just wouldn't do that sort of thing. Sure, she was fiercely independent, but she *wasn't* cheap. He'd lied about her to protect himself.

I had a duty to see that he didn't spread any of those filthy lies around the town, and if I was smashed to bits at the bottom of the cliff I wouldn't be too effective. I knew it wouldn't be easy to counteract Dewie's stories about Marty. From what he had said, my presence wasn't exactly charismatic. I'd tried so hard to be "one of the guys" and all I'd accomplished was to make myself look foolish and indirectly put my sister in a coma.

Boy, was I screwed up! My values were so mixed up that it would take a decade to sort them out. Well, maybe only a year or so. But at least I was starting. I put the car in reverse and backed down the hill to the road.

Sixteen

W hen I drove up to the curb Dad came rushing out of the house and down to the car.

I climbed out and came around to meet him. Without a word he put his arms around me and held me to him. Then, brushing his hand across his eyes, he took me by the arm and led me into the house.

When we were seated across from each other, he spoke.

"I won't ask where you've been, Joe, and you don't need to tell me. I know you well enough to know you've done nothing wrong. I'm only glad you're back home. I need you very much right now."

I don't think Dad had ever called me Joe before in my entire life. It made more impact on me than anything else he said. I have to admit I was closer to blubbering like a baby than I had been since I started kindergarten.

I tried to speak, feeling I owed him some sort of explanation. "I was going to . . ." I began hesitantly.

He put up his hand to stop me. "No, I meant what I said." He leaned back on the couch and studied me for a moment. Then, his voice thick with emotion, he said,

"Joe, I've been thinking a great deal about what you told us at the hospital."

Here it comes, I thought, the blast I so richly deserve. I was almost welcoming it. But I was wrong.

"First," he continued, "I want you to know that as far as I'm concerned everything you told us about your actions over the past few weeks is history. I have no intentions of punishing you or criticizing you or lecturing you on your behavior. I'm sure anything I could say to you would be mild compared to what you are saying to yourself.

"Second, I want you to rid your mind of any guilt you might have regarding Marty's accident. We both know your sister very well. She would have found some way to get to that party whether you helped her or not. And you certainly can't be responsible for her choosing to drive with a boy who had been drinking. When Marty is well and home again we'll all take a good look at what's been happening. I see that I'm going to have to make a few changes in my own attitude, and I'll expect you and Marty to do the same."

He stood up and looked down at me. "You're a good son, Joseph. I wonder if I've been such a good father."

He left the room before I could form an answer.

I sat there on the chair trying to fit all the pieces together. How could he forgive me and call me a good son after what I'd done. He just didn't seem to understand the whole ugly mess. I should have told him what I'd almost done to Dewie, but I don't suppose he would have ever understood that either.

I figured my father must be one of those people who aren't really of this world. He couldn't realize or accept that most of the time people are less than angelic. He

just went around with his head in the clouds, preaching
his sermons on Sundays and exuding sweetness and
light without having any idea what was really going on
in the world. I suppose that's what Dewie meant when
he said Dad was a joke in the town. I loved him very
much at that moment, but I realized that I was finding
it hard to really respect him. I sighed. "It's like
everyone says," I muttered to myself, "nice guys finish
last."

A moment later the doorbell rang. It was Mrs.
Granger with a covered casserole and a salad. She was
followed almost immediately by the Rutlands from
next door with a couple of pies.

Half an hour later Woody arrived at the door.

"You okay?" he asked, peering anxiously at me.

"Yeah, I'm okay," I answered, moving aside to let
him in.

He gave me another piercing look, then nodded,
turned, and went back down the steps. I silently
thanked him for not asking why I'd left the A & W in
such a rush and where I'd gone. I sometimes think
Woody knows me better than I know myself.

* * *

The rest of the week managed to go by without my
being conscious of anything but Marty and my folks.
Mom spent every day at the hospital and Dad was there
all night. The nurses set up a cot for him so he could
stay right in the room with her. He still insisted on
carrying on with his parish duties — visiting the sick,
comforting the bereaved, all that stuff that he considered to be so momentous. I'm sure the whole town
thought he was either nuts or totally stunned the way

he was acting as though his so-called duties were so important when his only daughter was maybe dying in the hospital.

One thing about that week that was positive, though. Dad and I got around to doing a lot of talking. We didn't discuss the things that had happened in the past week at all. Mostly we talked about when Marty and I were kids. He remembered so many funny stories that I'd completely forgotten. He also told me a lot of stuff about his own childhood: how his father had been a minister of a very large city church and how he, my father, had been expected to follow in his footsteps.

"I tell you, Joseph, the thought of it scared me half to death," he confessed one evening when we were sitting around after dinner, drinking lukewarm tea. "I was such a shy boy, I literally lost my lunch every time I was asked to recite in class." He laughed uproariously. "I decided when it was time to go to university that I'd run off to Toronto and be a clown. I could hide behind the makeup and no one would know who I was."

"Why didn't you?" I asked, thinking that the story reminded me of something.

"Well, I thought I'd better give university a one-year try just to please the old man. Then I discovered I loved it so much that I just stayed on. By the time I graduated I knew that I wanted to be a minister too. Not like my father though, I'm afraid. I wasn't interested in the big parish. I wanted to find a small town where I thought I could do some good. So when I left divinity school I was offered the church here and I've been in Hubank ever since."

It was a sad and touching story. Dad, I knew, was a very smart man. Yet here he was almost fifty years old and all he had to show for his life was a twenty-year hitch at a nothing church in a town nobody outside a radius of a hundred miles had ever heard of.

I kept waiting to hear that Mr. Riceman's lawyer had been in touch with Dad and was filing assault charges against me; however, it never happened. I wanted to talk to Dad about it, but the couple of times I tried to broach the subject he began talking about something else. I have to admit I didn't push it. I really wasn't too proud of what I had nearly done to Dewie, and Dad and I were getting along so well that I hated to spoil it.

Things weren't nearly so good at school, though. I kept away from the cafeteria at lunch so I wouldn't have to run into any of my fraternity brothers. Every time I thought about how they pledged me just so they could raise their academic standards, I wanted to hide in a closet. Oh, sure, most of them made an effort to come up to me and offer their condolences about Marty, but that didn't take the sting out of what they had done.

Then there was Amy. She phoned a couple of times, but I was out and never returned her calls. I knew she was concerned, but I just didn't want to talk to anyone — not even her.

I went to the hospital every afternoon when school was out to spell Mom off so she could go to the cafeteria and get herself some dinner. Every day I sat on Marty's bed and talked to her, telling her what had happened at school, read her the cards that had come for her, related some of Dad's stories. She just lay there not moving, not indicating in any way that she heard a word I'd said. I'd come away from the hospital every day feeling such pain that I didn't know how I was going to bear it. Then I'd get home, eat dinner, and talk to Dad, and pretty soon the pain would leave.

The only person I couldn't avoid was Woody. He

stuck to me like Saran Wrap whenever we had classes together as well as noon and after school. I didn't do much talking, I guess, other than to ask him if Dewie was spreading any rumors about Marty. That was my only concern right then.

"No way, Joe," he assured me. "In fact, no one's seen Dewie Riceman since last Monday. The word is his dad has taken him out of school and sent him off to relatives somewhere back east."

As least that was one thing I didn't have to worry about. I was still pretty certain his father was going to take me to court, but that I could handle when and if it ever happened.

* * *

On Friday when she came back from eating, Mom told me that I was to join the band for the Elks dance on Saturday. She wouldn't take no for an answer.

"You can't accomplish anything by sitting around the house, Joe. And you've worked so hard that it would be a shame to miss it. Besides, the rest of the group is depending on you."

When I told Gord on Saturday morning that I'd be playing that night, he couldn't keep the relief out of his voice.

"Gee, Joe, are you sure? We'd understand if you didn't want to make it."

"I know you would. But letting you guys down isn't going to make Marty well. So I'll see you at eight. And, Gord, I'm sorry about missing so many practices. It won't happen again."

"Forget it, Joe. You're so good you don't need to practice."

That wasn't true, but it was nice of him to say it anyway.

* * *

On Saturday I went down to the grocery store to do my deliveries. Mr. Granger was surprised to see me, but he had the sense not to make a big deal out of it.

"Glad you could make it, Joe," he said when I came in about ten o'clock. "Here's your list."

Everywhere I went with my deliveries people asked about Marty and wanted to know what they could do to help. Our town isn't huge, but it's not a wide spot in the road either. I was amazed at how many people knew about Marty, people I hardly knew myself.

* * *

I finished up about five and hurried home where I had a quick supper, a shower, and a change of clothes. Then before going on to the dance I went over to the hospital to spell Mom off and spend an hour or so with Marty. When I rushed into the room, I saw Amy sitting in a chair talking to Mom. Finding her there was totally unexpected.

"Amy, what are you doing here?" I asked, then realized how stupid that sounded.

She smiled and said, "Keeping your mom company."

"She's been here every evening, Joe. I thought you knew," Mom added.

I hadn't, of course. It was just one more thing I was finding out about my family and friends. I guess I'd always thought of Amy as a little self-centered. Kind and generous, but not really concerned about anything more serious than having a good time and her music.

Oh, she was fun and exciting, but not the kind of girl I thought would be spending every evening sitting with a grieving mother. And I was still thinking that what Dewie said about her going out with me for laughs was true. I wondered if I was *ever* going to understand people — especially one, Joe Larriby.

I stared at her without speaking, my mouth hanging attractively open.

"Your mom tells me you're going to be playing at the dance. That's good," she said, sounding embarrassed.

"I guess. I sure don't want to let the band down, but somehow it doesn't seem right for me to be whooping it up while Marty is lying there looking so . . ."

"You know that Marty wouldn't want you to miss the dance, Joe," Mom said. "I'll be here all night with her, and your father will be joining me as soon as he finishes writing his sermon for tomorrow morning."

"Dad's going to preach tomorrow?" I couldn't believe it.

"Of course he is. It's his job."

"But no one will expect him to conduct a church service after what's happened."

"Maybe not, but your father expects it of himself. He believes very much in what he does, Joe, although I know you find that hard to understand."

That was the understatement of the decade, but I sure wasn't about to let Mom know how I felt.

"So you two better scoot. I'll see you tomorrow."

Amy and I left her sitting beside Marty's bed, holding her daughter's hand and quietly smiling to herself.

Seventeen

The hall was packed. Most of the people were in costume, but there were a few of the older folks in suits and evening dresses. The place was decorated in the traditional orange and black of Halloween with cut-outs of witches on brooms, black cats, and goblins everywhere. Tables for six or eight people surrounded the dance floor, and the bar and buffet table took up the whole north end of the room. The band was on the stage at the south end. Nearly everyone was dancing, or trying to in the limited space.

It was ten-thirty and the band was taking a break. Amy and I left to get a drink and something to eat, but the others stayed on stage. People were milling around the food tables and drifting back to their tables when Mr. Bryce, the program guy from the Elks Club who had listened to us play way back when, picked up the mike and called for attention.

"While you're catching your breath from all that dancing, we have a special treat for you. The young man you are going to see is just beginning his career, but we predict great things for him. We saw him first on a kiddies' show on Channel 10 and asked him if he would consent to give us a sample of his act here tonight. He very graciously agreed. May I present our city's answer to Marcel Marceau: Wilfred "Woody" Albert!"

Gord gave a drumroll and Woody leaped out from the wings onto the stage. He was dressed entirely in black: jeans, turtleneck sweater, sneakers, and cap. The white paint on his face was a startling contrast.

I'd seen Woody perform for kids many times and I knew how good he was. But I'd never seen him work an adult audience. Instead of telling the people what he was going to do, the way he did with children, he went directly into his routine without a word of explanation.

He was amazing.

His first mime was a guy opening a cereal box and pouring himself breakfast. You knew without a doubt what he was doing from the minute he started trying to get his fingers under the tabs to open the new box to having it explode all over the floor. When he was finished his first routine, the whole hall was on its feet.

He did a couple more: a very inexperienced steno trying to type from his shorthand notes and a tailor measuring an overweight, fussy customer. At the end of his act, the audience applauded for about five minutes. He did a pantomime of a prima donna taking a bow and swept off into the wings.

Amy and I ran to the back of the stage where a dressing room had been hastily erected. We found Woody sitting calmly in front of a mirror removing his makeup and whistling to himself.

"Man, you were sensational!" I cried. "I had no idea you did anything but routines for kids."

"He's right," Amy affirmed. "You were just marvelous."

Woody just sat there peering nearsightedly in the mirror and mopping off white paint.

"Why didn't you tell me you were going to be performing tonight?"

"It's no big deal," he answered. "I'm not sure they even liked me."

"Liked you? They practically ate you up! Now move it and get that stuff off," I urged. "Everyone's out there waiting to congratulate you."

The whistling stopped and he looked pleadingly at me in the mirror.

"I'm not going out there, Joe. I couldn't face all those people. I'd die of embarrassment."

"Woody, you just faced 'all those people' on stage for fifteen minutes. What are you talking about?"

"I can do anything when I'm behind this white paint, Joe. You know that. But with my bare face I go all to pieces."

"Well, that's not going to happen this time," Amy declared. "Now put that tissue down and get moving."

He wiped off the last of the cold cream, put on his glasses, and muttered, "No way!"

Then before he had a chance to dig in his heels she had him by the arm and was propelling him out the door and into the crowded hall. Immediately he was surrounded by a group of gushing fans. I could see how uncomfortable he was and started to go to his rescue, but Amy held me back.

"Leave him alone, Joe. He'll be fine when he realizes he doesn't have to do anything but bask in the glory. It'll do him nothing but good."

She was right, of course. When he finally broke away from the crowd and came over to where Amy and I were watching him, he was grinning from ear to ear.

"I've had three offers to do my act here in town, Joe!" he exclaimed. "And a guy from the city wants me for the big Remembrance Day telethon next month. I'll be on national TV! Can you believe it?"

"Without any trouble," I answered, grinning back at him. "I always knew you had star genes hidden away somewhere."

Amy reached up and kissed him on the cheek. "Maybe we can double-date again sometime, Woody. I really do have a few tame girlfriends!"

Woody just stood there blushing, alternately gazing in awe at Amy and checking out a group of girls standing across the room staring at him.

We left him, still stunned by his triumph, to go back to where the band was tuning up. I think I felt as thrilled over Woody's success as he did.

* * *

It was after one when the dance finally ended and we were able to pack up our instruments and leave. Mr. Bryce came over to us and said a lot of nice things about our performance. Then he reached into his pocket and handed Gord a check.

"You'll find that the amount is a little different from what we agreed upon. However, I think it's a fair price."

Ellis and Mac both shrugged. I knew how they felt; just because we were kids he thought he could get away from paying us the agreed-upon fee. But we were wrong.

When he'd left Gord looked at the check and whistled.

"Wow, at this rate we can all retire before we graduate!"

When I saw what my share would be I knew I didn't have to rely on my job at Granger's Grocery any longer. He'd added an extra twenty percent to the fee.

Gord made a halfhearted suggestion that we all go out for burgers to celebrate, but no one took him up on it. We were all too tired both from the excitement of our first big performance and the actual work of playing almost nonstop for five hours.

Woody had stuck around till the end, still riding high on his showbiz triumph. I'd noticed a number of girls come over and ask him to dance during the evening, but he must have found some excuse to turn them down. I guess he wasn't ready for anything that intimate quite yet.

He had his mom's car and offered to drive Amy and me home. We'd walked over from the hospital, which was only a few blocks away, and didn't have transportation.

"You take Amy, Woody," I suggested. "I think I'd like to stop at the hospital to see Marty."

"Isn't it awfully late for you to be making a visit?" Woody asked.

"Yeah, but that's okay. The family has permission to see her anytime. She's in a private room, so we don't disturb anyone."

"Well, okay, if that's what you want." He looked a little dismayed about the prospect of having to be alone with Amy for the whole ten minutes it would take to drive her home, but I figured — as Amy would say —

it would do him nothing but good. "I can drop you at the hospital if you like," he added hopefully.

"Not necessary. It's out of your way, and it's only a couple of blocks. The walk'll do me good."

I walked them to the car and while Woody was opening his door I gave Amy a quick kiss.

"I'll call you tomorrow," I said. "And thanks for everything. Take good care of my friend."

Amy nodded. "I sure will." Then as she climbed into the car she murmured, "I'm sure I can find a nice girl for him."

"Oh, no. Please don't," Woody pleaded as he started the engine. "I couldn't handle another Cookie jar!"

I groaned and closed Amy's door.

* * *

Mom was asleep in the big chair by the window when I came into Marty's room. She half roused when she heard me and muttered, "Joe? Is that you?"

"Yeah, it's me, Mom. I thought I'd sit here with Marty for a few minutes. Did Dad go home?"

"Mmmm. A little while ago. Did you have a good time?"

I started to answer her but barely got launched on Woody's success when I saw she was fast asleep.

I pulled a blanket over her, then went to sit on Marty's bed. She looked so little lying there, her head in its huge bandage and the tubes sticking out of her arms. I took her hand and started to talk to her.

"Marty, it's Joe. I just got back from the dance; you remember, the Elks Halloween dance that Dad was so shook up about. Well, we were a big success, but not anything like the success Woody had."

I went on to describe Woody's performance and how he had been offered a spot on the telethon. "So you'll just have to get better so you can catch his TV debut."

Tears started to well up in my eyes as I wondered if Marty would ever watch TV again. It was a week now and there was no sign of her ever coming out of her coma. I thought about stories I'd heard of people who had been in comas for years. I didn't think I could stand it if that happened to Marty.

I bent over and kissed her cheek. "Please, Marty, if you can hear me, don't give up. Come back to us. We need you so much."

I looked at her face. There was still no sign she'd heard a word I'd said.

Eighteen

Much as I didn't want to, I got up to go to church with Dad the next morning. Mom took his place and stayed with Marty all night so he could have a good night's sleep before delivering his sermon. I don't think he had much of a sleep, though; I could hear him pacing up and down in his room most of the night.

Dr. Barker was getting pretty worried. Marty was still in a coma and showing no signs of coming out of it. I was secretly scared to death she never would, but both Mom and Dad were totally optimistic. Faith and all that stuff.

Anyway, I knew how important it was for me to be with him at church, so I made the big effort to pry myself out of bed after what seemed like about ten minutes sleep and staggered down to the kitchen to make breakfast.

"How did the dance go?" Dad asked as he poured out two cups of coffee and handed one over to me.

"Great," I answered, and proceeded to tell him about the guy giving us the extra fee and maybe our getting more well-paying jobs.

"And you should have seen Woody, Dad. He was sensational — had them rolling in the aisles. You'd never have recognized him. You know, shy old Woody — scared to speak to more than two people at once. Well, I tell you, when he got behind that white face he was a different person." I stopped dead. Dad was chuckling to himself. I looked over at him. Now I remembered why Dad's story about wanting to become a clown had such a familiar ring. He was another Woody. I started to laugh.

"Hey, that's why you've always thought Woody was so great," I accused him. "He's just like you."

"I admit I do see a little of myself in the boy," he answered, still chuckling. "Although I must admit I've never caused a traffic jam with a load of pumpkins." He drained the last of his coffee and stood up. "Better be on our way, son. I want to be sure everything is set up all right. Stan was planning to go to a party last night, and I don't suppose he's feeling too frisky this morning."

I finished my coffee and joined him. As we walked the few blocks to the church, I wondered what my life would have been like if Dad *had* joined the circus.

* * *

When we got home a little after two, Dad sort of staggered into the house and fell onto a chair without even taking off his coat.

"I'll just rest for a moment, then be off to the hospital to relieve your mother," he explained, leaning his head wearily against the back of the chair. I looked down at him. His eyes were closed and his skin was the color of putty. He looked exhausted. In less than a minute he was fast asleep. I picked up an afghan from the couch and threw it over him, then slipped quietly out of the room.

I was in the kitchen heating up a piece of leftover pizza when I heard a knock on the back door. I expected it to be another pie or casserole but it wasn't food — it was Woody.

"Come on," he ordered as he flung the door open. "We're going over to the Elks Hall."

"I've been to the Elks Hall," I answered, taking a big bite of pizza and burning my tongue. "Ow, that's hot!" I yelled.

"Serves you right for being such a pig," Woody said, grinning. "Now get moving. We haven't got all day."

"Look, Woody," I sighed, "I know you're trying to get me to relax a little, but I'm really not in the mood to be around people. Besides, the hospital might phone about Marty and I'd miss the call. Dad's dead to the world in the living room. I don't think he'd hear it if a jet landed on the piano."

"My father let me have the car; it's out front. Here's your jacket," he said and shoved me out the door.

Apparently he wasn't taking no for an answer. Well, maybe he's right, I thought. I was beginning to get awfully tired of sitting around the house waiting for news that never came.

"What going on at the Elks anyway?" I asked, only mildly curious as I shrugged into my jacket and followed him around to the front of the house. "It must be something for your dad to let you drive his precious BMW."

"It is. Now get in."

When we drove into the parking lot, I was surprised at the number of cars that were already there. Woody managed to squeeze the BMW into a narrow spot against the building, missing the Chevy beside us by millimeters. Woody opened his door and we both got out on his side.

When we came into the hall I was astonished to see it was packed with people. All the folding chairs were filled and people were lined up along the walls. Mr. Granger was at a mike at the front of the room talking.

"You all know why we're here. Marty Larriby is in hospital in a coma. We are all friends of the Larribys; some of us have known Rupert and Marcella since before they were married. We have watched Marty grow into the lovely young lady she is today, and we want to do what we can to help her."

He paused and looked around the room.

"I suggest we have fifteen minutes of silence while we all turn our loving thoughts to the Larriby family and send out our positive affirmations for Marty's complete recovery. After that, anyone who wants to say anything may come up and speak."

At once the room was silent. I looked around in amazement as people I barely knew closed their eyes and bowed their heads.

"What's going on, Woody?" I whispered.

"It's an old-fashioned love-in, Joe. The Grangers and Hubanks organized it. The idea is for everyone to put their whole conscious thinking into Marty getting well. It's been done thousands of times before with some-times amazing results."

After a minute or two, I was beginning to think he might be right. The energy in the room was strong enough to light up half the houses in the city. I looked around at the crowd and was astonished to see nearly all my frat brothers, some sitting with their parents, others in a group of other kids from school. As a matter of fact, most of the kids in my class were there, as well as a number of the teachers. There was also a large contingent of eighth graders, Marty's classmates. I was flabbergasted. I would have expected Marty's classmates to be there, but the fact that so many of my own fellow students had shown up just about blew my mind.

When the fifteen minutes were up, Mr. Granger asked, "Does anyone have anything they want to say?"

A young woman I'd seen around but didn't know by name got up and came to the front of the room.

"I'd just like to tell you about the time my baby was very sick and Dr. Larriby stayed with us all night at the hospital. He was so positive that she would get well and so comforting. When my little girl recovered, the doctor said it was just as much Dr. Larriby's doing as his. I'll be grateful to him for the rest of my life."

She sat down and old Mrs. Walters took her place.

"Dr. Larriby was with me when my Will died," she said. "I was so grieved I was unable to function. As you may know, Will and I had no family, but Dr. Larriby stayed with me and took care of all the details — notifying friends, the funeral arrangements, everything. I couldn't have managed without him."

When she had finished, she handed the mike to a guy about my age.

"When I got busted for hot-wiring a car, Dr. Larriby came to my trial. He spoke up for me, even though he didn't really know me that well. As a result I was given a suspended sentence and put into his custody. Every week, regular as sunrise, he came over to the house and we talked. He got me into a training program at the tech and even managed to pry a bursary out of the school to help me out. If it wasn't for Dr. Larriby I'd probably be doing time right now."

It went on like this for another forty-five minutes — people getting up and telling the audience how great my father is. Nobody ever mentioned the church at all. To these people Dad was a friend when they needed a friend most. Now he needed them, and they were there to give him their total support.

On the drive home Woody didn't speak; nor did I. When we got to the house I asked him to come in, but I guess he knew I wanted to be alone.

"I'll call you tomorrow, Joe," he said. "If you need me, you know my number."

"Yeah, thanks, Woody. And thanks for taking me to the hall tonight. It was quite an experience."

"It was, wasn't it. Quite a guy, your old man."

"Yeah," I muttered as he drove off. "Quite a guy."

Dad was just as I'd left him, sound asleep in the chair. I figured he needed as much sleep as he could get and decided to go myself to the hospital to relieve Mom. I wrote him a quick note telling him where I was, left it on the table beside him and, taking the keys from his jacket pocket, slipped back out the door.

Mom was sitting in her usual chair beside Marty, holding her hand and singing softly to her.

"Joe, dear, where's your father?" she asked as I came in the room.

"Sound asleep in his recliner," I told her. "I'm here to relieve you."

I was still reeling from the experience at the Elks Hall. I'd thought about it all the way to the hospital. Those people really believed that somehow their combined love could heal Marty. It was amazing! I didn't believe it for one minute, but that wasn't what was causing my mind to go tilt. It was the way they spoke of my father. They didn't see him as a loser at all. In fact, they seemed to think he was some sort of saint. I didn't understand, but I knew I had to tell Mom about it before I exploded.

I went over everything that had happened: the lady with the sick baby, old Mrs. Walters, the kid in court, all of it. I described how the whole packed auditorium became completely still while everyone sent out loving thoughts to Marty and then how the room was suddenly filled with energy.

That about did her in. She'd been so controlled through this whole ordeal, never crying — at least not in front of anyone — always optimistic, never giving in to her fears. But when I finished recounting all the stuff the people had said about Dad, she started sobbing and didn't stop for a good ten minutes. I decided it was long overdue and let her cry herself out, saying nothing, just holding her and passing the Kleenex.

When she'd dried her eyes, she sat up and smiled at me.

"Thank you for telling me about it, Joe. I wish I could have been there to hear it for myself, but on the other hand, I'm sure they didn't say anything I haven't always known about your father."

I just nodded. There was no way I was going to tell her how completely surprised I'd been. I'm sure she thought I'd always considered my father a success in his work, whereas I'd figured him to be a loser — a nice, lovable, innocent loser. Marty's accident, tragic though it was, at least had the effect of bringing me to my senses about my dad.

"I guess maybe I'll slip down and get myself a cup of tea and some toast, Joe." She got up and and came over to kiss me. "I'll be back in a few minutes."

When she left I went over and sat on the bed beside

Marty. I took her hand the way I always do and started talking to her.

"Boy, I sure have been wrong about Dad. I guess I've been wrong about a lot of things, Marty." I could feel the tears starting to form behind my eyes. I was glad no one was watching as I let them pour out. "Oh, how I wish you could have heard what I told Mom about the love-in. I wish you could hear me tell you how much everyone loves you — especially me. Oh, Marty, I wish you could hear me!"

I looked down at her face. It was entirely expressionless. Nothing moved. Nothing showed any signs of life.

Then I felt it: a slight but definite pressure on my hand.

Nineteen

I wish I could say that Marty suddenly opened her eyes and smiled at me. Or that she made a sudden recovery and was back to school the next week. Those things only happen in soap operas, I guess. No, she's still in hospital, but the doctors say she's going to be okay. It's just a matter of time. She is awake and seems to be aware of what's going on around her, but she isn't speaking yet. Dr. Barker said it would still be a while before she's her old self again. I don't suppose she'll ever be her *old* self. Neither will I. But I can't help but believe we'll both be even better.

I've thought so much over the past few weeks about that love-in at the Elks Hall. It *did* seem like a miracle, but who's to know for sure? Marty might have been going to come out of the coma anyway. But way back in the far recesses of my mind I can't help believe that the energy I felt in the room that afternoon had a power I'll never understand. And somehow I know that power is still working to make Marty recover fully.

We arranged to have a TV set put in Marty's room on Remembrance Day so we could all watch Woody do his stuff on the telethon. He knocked 'em dead, as usual. I watched Marty while she watched Woody and

I cried inside when I saw her smile at a couple of things he did.

It's funny about Woody. Ever since his big success at the Halloween dance, he's really come out of himself. For the first time since I've known him he's been comfortable talking to people.

I'm still with the band, of course. We're really doing well too. The Halloween dance did just what Gord predicted it would. We're booked nearly every weekend until Christmas. As a matter of fact, Mom managed to persuade Dad to come to one of the dances where we were playing. He was obviously very impressed and a little surprised that we were as good as we were. It made me feel really great, even though he kept coming up to the bandstand and requesting numbers written back in the middle ages — like "Stardust" — and causing Mac and Ellis to practically dislocate their shoulders.

We don't practice every night the way we did when we were getting ready for the Elks dance, so I'm going to choir practice again. I really like choir, so it's no big sacrifice, although even if it were a chore I'd still do it for Dad's sake.

Dad and I had a serious talk about changes we both needed to make and got a lot of stuff sorted out. We both admitted we'd made some pretty stupid mistakes and ended up doing a lot of sensible compromising. I don't go to Young People's but I've taken over as leader of a Cub group, which is terrific.

I've given up my job with Mr. Granger. The band often has Friday-night bookings and it's so late when I get home that getting up to go to work is too much since we often have to play Saturday night as well. But it's not a problem financially because the band gets paid very well and I make a lot more than I did delivering groceries.

Amy and I manage to get together alone about once a week, which doesn't seem like much, I guess. But we're together when the band is playing a dance or house party. I told her what Dewie had said about her and me, and I thought she was going to go into cardiac arrest.

"That pimply-faced little piece of pond scum!" she cried. "How dare he spread lies like that!" She paused and looked queerly at me. "You didn't believe him, did you?"

"Of course not," I lied, feeling a little foolish but stupidly happy.

Incidentally, Mr. Riceman's lawyer never did contact us about my assault on Dewie. I guess he figured he had his hands full getting Dewie off on all the charges the police threw at him. It couldn't have happened to a nicer guy.

I didn't quit the fraternity, though I gave it a lot of thought before I made my decision. I talked it over with Cliff, trying to get him to admit that they had pledged me because of my grades, and found out that the story was just another of Dewie Riceman's fabrications. But it wasn't finding that out that made me decide to stay. Nor was it based on what Amy wanted me to do. If I had quit, I like to think she'd still want to go steady with me, but that doesn't really matter. I stayed with the fraternity for a couple of reasons: first, because I still have this need to feel I'm part of a group of guys I really like. I guess the seventeen years when I was an outsider are still taking their toll. Maybe someday I'll be mature enough, sure enough of myself, that I won't need group support. But I'm not there yet.

The other reason is that I made a couple of promises to my brothers when I joined the fraternity and I intend to honor them. I've had enough of lies and deceit and not keeping my word.

I brought Woody's name up again for membership and this time it was greeted with cheers. Woody, however, declined the invitation.

"It's just not for me, Joe," he told me. "Those guys are into things that just don't interest me. I'd be a drag."

I tried to talk him into it, but it was useless. Maybe it's just as well; he's busy all the time nowadays with his performances. He added a number of new twists to his regular mime act: juggling, a few magic tricks, that sort of thing.

Also, he's got a girlfriend, if you can believe it. No, not someone Amy found for him; he got her all on his own. She's in grade 11 — quiet, shy, a big chess buff. She and Woody have doubled with Amy and me a couple of times, and it's been really good.

In fact, Woody and I see each other almost as much as we did way back last year. Only now we really have something positive in common, both being performers, instead of being losers like before. We talk a lot about what we'll do with ourselves when we finish high school. Woody wants to study mime seriously and I'd like to get a music degree. Dad is still hoping I'll go into the ministry, but I just don't think I have the calling — at least not at this point in my life.

Otherwise, things go on pretty much the same. On the surface, at least. Mrs. Granger still brings us mysterious casseroles; Saralee Tidbell still fawns whenever we meet; Mac and Ellis still communicate with their shoulders; Stan still moons the Ladies Aid.

But nothing is really the same as it was way back last summer. And I know it never will be again.

I guess that's okay too.

DUE

Printed in Canada